WIT~~HOUT~~

a

SHADOW

OTHER BOOKS AND AUDIOBOOKS
BY BRETT CAIN

Frank Sawyer Series
Whiteout
Out by Night
Without a Shadow

Brett Cain

In Memoriam

Dave Knapp, a worthy husband and father
&
Bonnie Brown, who all her life scattered sunshine

ACKNOWLEDGMENTS

This book would not be possible without you. You are now as committed to this journey as I am and as our characters are. There is much to be said about creating content, whether it be a blog, a vlog, a YouTube channel, or a simple book. I am a firm believer that everyone can and should write and if you want to write, you must read.

I am very grateful to Joe Pemberton, the brains and brawn behind Nauvoo Supply Company who reached out to me when my previous publisher set me adrift.

I would have long-since stopped trying my hand at this craft if it were not for Kevin Dolan and all the men behind EXIT.ORG who have been a constant source of inspiration and discipline.

Many other anonymous writer friends have buyoued me up whenever I have found myself weighed down. You know who you are.

My family has never let me quit and they have never quit on me.

This story is different from my previous books in that Sawyer deals with some more existential questions, about what is real and what is not, about what matters and what doesn't. Dreams have been a permanent fixture in my own life and, beyond dreams, faith. Whether or not you believe in God, the devil, Heaven or hell, my hope is that this book will at least give you reason to believe in yourself.

So once again, the best compliment I can give every one of you is just this; Thank you.

CHAPTER ONE

I had never been to Girls' Camp. Mainly on account of my not being a girl. Manliness notwithstanding, my sweetheart and San Diego County Sheriff's Deputy, Melanie Clark, had invited me to come speak to the young women from Church about my missionary service to Peru.

After our adventure last fall, I had decided to stick around in the town of Cesar, working through the winter at a variety of casual labor jobs. I had repeatedly and emphatically declined Melanie's offers to put in a word for me with the Sheriff's Department. It was a "thanks, but no thanks" kind of thing. I wanted to be able to operate outside the confines of the law. If I took a job like that, I would have to fill out all kinds of paperwork, which was about as appealing as a root canal.

Last month, Melanie got baptized and was now serving in the congregation as the Young Women's president. It was summer, and with school out, her Church assignment had taken a lot more of her time. Fortunately, crime in Cesar seemed to have taken a well-timed sabbatical and with the exception of a few overly enthusiastic motorists, things had been peaceful.

In years past, the ward had held summer camps at a Church-owned site, but that location was undergoing some renovations, and we needed a new venue. This group of girls was much smaller than was typical for a Church Girls' Camp. There were only nine young women, Melanie, and me. A senior missionary couple, Brother and Sister Ayres, caravanned with us, their rig loaded down with supplies.

We drove for several winding miles on lonely highways until we began a slow, ponderous course through thick woods, across narrow bridges, and roller coasting along steep unpaved roads. All the while getting deeper into the Southern California mountains. The teenage girls sang and chattered, danced, and snacked in the back of the fifteen-passenger van.

Only a couple of hours from civilization, we were still remarkably remote, which suited me just fine. I love to camp. I love being out of doors. But after the first mile on the dirt tracks, the girls started protesting at the loss of cell-service. Melanie, like me, was a firm believer in the spirit of the law more than the letter and had, against tradition, allowed the girls to retain their smartphones.

We had driven up, around, and over tall ridges, descending into a heavily wooded valley, surrounded by craggy peaks on every side. The valley reminded me of the inside of a volcano, except instead of lava bubbling at the center there was a cerulean lake.

As we got nearer to the lakeside, the road became more rutted and overgrown with weeds and grass.

An artful, if weather-beaten, sign at the edge of the campsite announced "Ghost Lake". The letters looked as if they had been burnt into the wood with a hot poker, giving it a rustic and semi-spooky feel.

One of the girls, Kaytee, I think, asked, "Why is it called Ghost Lake?"

Another of the teens, Emeline, made an "oooo" sound and wiggled her fingers dramatically, giving rise to a chorus of laughter from the others.

Melanie smiled her starry smile, glancing in the rearview mirror. "More like *Holy* Ghost Lake now that we're here."

Kaytee was persistent, "No, really, why's it called that?"

Melanie shrugged, "I'm not sure."

"I guess we'll find out tonight, am I right?" said another girl, Aubrey, elbowing her neighbor and pretending her fingers were the spectral digits of some witch like Emeline had.

"There's no such thing as ghosts. According to Cahuilla legend, this was one of the places Tahquitz, an evil spirit, hunted for people's souls. He was said to appear as a green meteor."

The girls were quiet, looking at me strangely.

Melanie raised an elegant eyebrow at me.

I shrugged. "I did a little research on the place." Turning back to the girls, I continued, "like I said, there's no such thing as ghosts. The water is very cold, though, even in summer, so stay with a swim buddy and not too far from shore. Hypothermia can set in before you know it, even during this time of year. Also, we will need to keep our eyes peeled for critters."

"*Critters*? Like, wild animals?" asked Ashlin, a fashionable and hip-looking kid who seemed the least inclined to roughing it. One of the other girls, probably Taylor, made a soft roaring sound and grabbed Ashlin's shoulder like the talons of a hawk. They screamed and laughed and forgot all about animals and ghosts and lakes and ambient temperatures.

Melanie came to a stop at the center of the camp. The Ayres parked beside us. The place looked pretty run-down, which I should have expected. It had been the only campground without exorbitant prices per night or extensive waitlists.

Melanie and I exchanged a look, anticipating groans from the girls, but, surprisingly, they didn't seem to mind the more rustic conditions.

Sister Ayres appeared at Melanie's window, tapping on the glass.

Cranking down her window, Melanie looked apologetically at the older woman. Sister Ayres smiled, adjusting her glasses and stretching her arms out as if to say *isn't this magnificent?*

"I thought the accommodations would be better. I'm sorry, I had no idea."

Sister Ayres shook her head. "This is more like a five-star hotel than what we're used to when it comes to camping." Her voice was strong, feminine, without the tremulous quaver so common to women her age.

Sister Ayres clapped her hands. "All right, girls, let's all get on out. Brother Sawyer isn't going to carry all your bags, though I'm sure he could if he wanted to." She smiled at me.

I smiled back and flexed my arms comically.

I never got tired of seeing that smile.

The Ayres, for some far-too-generous reason, were fond of me, and I of them. I had never got to know my own grandparents and the Ayres seemed straight out of a storybook. Like Mr. and Mrs. Claus or something.

They practically doted over Melanie. Even more than I did, if that were possible.

Not that she needed doting on.

The young women tumbled out of the van, eager to stretch their legs and have a look around.

The layout of the camp itself was a bit sparse but had been well-designed if not well-kept. A large main building sat on a concrete pad facing south towards the lake that was seventy-five yards down the forested slope. I could see a floating dock rocking in the wind and little lake waves.

There was a courtyard between the building and where we parked the vehicles. It looked like it could have been used as a sort of sports court, for pickleball or basketball, maybe, but there were no nets or hoops now.

The main building was flanked to the west by three cedar-shake cabins that formed three sides of a square. They were each labelled according to a cardinal direction. North, East, and West.

There was a spot for a fourth cabin closest to the lake, what would have presumably been the South. It was empty except for four concrete blocks. Perhaps the foundation for another, as-yet unbuilt structure, or one that had been torn down. With the general dilapidation, it seemed unlikely to be constructed or re-constructed any time soon.

All three cabins had a set of three wooden steps that led to a narrow door on either side of which were two small windows facing the lake.

On the southside of the main structure, I saw a flagpole. I looked up and realized that Old Glory was indeed old but didn't look all that glorious with faded colors and a frayed edge. It was also hanging upside down.

At least they have a flag, I thought.

While the girls explored each of the cabins, trying to stake claims to top bunks. I made my way to the mast to fix the flag.

"Where's the caretaker? He was going to meet us here, right?"

Melanie came through the lakeside door of the main building and looked around, and, as if on cue, from around west corner of the building appeared a man. He was a tall, middle-aged rangy fellow. He was wiping his hands across the front of a blue jumpsuit. Across his waist he wore a tool belt, and he was a few days from a shave and more than that from a haircut.

He smiled and waved at us, making his way over.

His voice had a slight Slavic taste to it. Maybe half a generation removed from the old country.

"I just finished with the kitchen. Not much to look at, but the water runs and the stove works—it just might take a while to get hot."

I pointed at the flag. "What happened there? It was upside down when we got here."

He looked up, shielding his eyes from the late afternoon sun filtering through the trees in a high-mountain breeze.

"That's the right way now, isn't it?"

"Yes. I fixed it."

He shrugged. "Must have been mistake."

"*A* mistake." I said, noting his lack of the article.

Melanie slapped my arm.

He didn't seem to catch my correction, nor Melanie's reprimand of me.

"I am Stanislav."

We shook hands and introduced ourselves.

"I live in trailer next to lake." He pointed past the cluster of buildings where the trees thinned along the shore. I couldn't see it from where I was standing.

"Please to be meeting you."

He left, hitching his tool belt, and whistling through his teeth.

I watched him go and I must have had a sour look on my face because Melanie, intuitive as ever, put a hand on my arm.

"You don't like him?"

"Who? Smirnoff? I don't mind him. I just don't like the flag being disrespected."

"His name is Stanislav."

"Whatever."

"You *are* in a mood. That's not like you at all." She said, softly, moving her hand from my arm to my shoulder.

I looked away but touched her hand with mine.

"I'm worried."

"Okay, that is *definitely* not like you, Mr. Indomitable." She said, gruffly, flexing out her arms like some macho strongman.

"It's just—these kids, and the Ayres, and you. It's a lot to worry about. I just want to keep everyone safe."

"Well, you don't have to worry about me, I'm a big girl." I hugged her. "Don't I know it."

With one arm around her, I held my left hand up, palm facing inward, fingers splayed. Wiggling my index finger, I indicated the white scar between the thumb and forefinger. It looked like the Cheshire Cat's smile, wide and curved upwards at the ends.

"I got that as a teenager, whittling."

I turned my hand over, balling all my fingers except the littlest. A vivid scar crossed diagonally under the knuckle.

"Machete." I said.

Swapping hands, I showed her a pinkish scar on my right palm. It looked like a flower beginning to bloom. "This was from accidentally resting my hand on one of those things you burn to keep the 'squitoes away."

The Ayres were walking back towards us, having overseen the unpacking and cabin assignments.

Melanie kissed my cheek. "I get it, you're wonderfully scarred and oh so manly. These girls aren't going to be whittling, we have bug spray. Everything's going to be fine. You just need to relax."

Her hand gingerly slid down my back, over the scar I had received from the knife of a human trafficker. "Or...are you still thinking about more recent injuries?"

I stepped away as the Ayres drew near, motioning us to the mess hall.

Holding a thumbs up to the older couple, I said out of the side of my mouth to Melanie. "No way. That's practically ancient history. That was the least worrisome of all my wounds I've ever had."

She shook her head and smiled.

I started unloading boxes of dry goods, pancake mixes, beans, cartons of eggs, milk, bacon, and other more basic elements of food.

Brother Ayres was, by many standards, a short man, but a spiritual giant, and his eyes were always smiling. He was wise and gentle, and I could not have asked for a better patriarch to have along.

While some of the girls might have been planning on "scary-stories-to-tell-in-the-dark", Brother Ayres was instead planning to rivet them with scripture stories, Church history, and practical Gospel instruction.

Sister Ayres inspected the kitchen as I emptied the contents of the boxes onto shelves, into cupboards, and the commercial refrigerator. She nodded approvingly, pulling on an apron.

"Was there any disagreement about who got which cabin?"

"Oh, no. The girls all get along splendidly. They didn't even seem to mind the cobwebs. Fresh air and sunshine will do wonders for them. No more looking at their screens, for a few days, anyway."

It was summer, and even though the days were long, the peaks soon blocked out the sun as it lowered in the sky.

Sister Ayres made what smelled like a delicious dinner, but I wasn't hungry. I walked around the grounds, finding the long dead remains of a few stone-ringed fire pits. I saw Stanislav's trailer, showing just a sliver of light shining out from between the curtains. He was some three hundred yards from the east cabin which was the furthest point of the campground.

I traced and retraced my way around the camp, from different angles, looking for any environmental hazards that the girls might trip over or run into during their games and activities.

The twilight sky was clear and even with no moon rising, I could see well. I walked up and down the dock, testing its stability. Like everything here, it needed work but seemed sturdy enough.

The lapping lake water sounded oddly subdued, as if the water noises were being muffled, drowned, and absorbed into the impossible depths of the night sky.

The tops of the mountains loomed like the spine of a dormant dragon, cutting out huge swathes of sky like those zig-zaggy safety scissors they give preschoolers for their construction paper.

I heard creaking on the dock and turned to see Melanie with a contingent of young women.

"Are you sure this is safe?" Melanie asked, toeing a loose board.

"Well, it's not getting any safer. It's holding me up and I weigh more than any two of you put together."

Some of the girls had an adventurous streak, wobbling and stamping their feet, causing the deck to shake like a skateboard over lumpy pavement. Waves rippled out from the dock, combating those from the soft breeze that rolled from the center of the lake.

Melanie cautioned them and I braced myself in case I had to dive in to rescue any of the daredevils. Fortunately, the dock held, and the girls kept their feet.

Aubrey, Olivia, Kaytee, and Kami had their arms full of the ingredients for s'mores.

"Brother Sawyer, can you light a fire for us, please?" Olivia asked.

"Sure, going to make s'mores, huh?" I said the name of the sweet treat just like Oliver Twist's famous line, *some more*.

Aubrey laughed, "it's pronounced *s'mores*, not *some oars*."

"But let's wait until we see a shooting star. When you're in town, you don't get to look that much at the sky and stars. Out here, though, they're always with us and much closer than you can imagine." I said.

Melanie, for once, didn't raise an eyebrow at my having waxed poetical. Instead, she took my hand and squeezed it gently.

We all looked up, turning this way and that, expectantly.

After a moment, Olivia pointed excitedly, "There's one!"

Kami tweaked her arm good-naturedly, "that's a satellite, silly."

After a while, the girls started rubbing their necks with the strain.

"Okay, everybody," I said, "we'll see one in, ten, nine, eight, seven, six, five, four, three, two—"

A tremendous streak of light flashed from one end of the heavens to the other. The biggest meteor I had ever seen, bigger than I could have imagined.

"Woah!" The girls said in unison.

Now Melanie raised an eyebrow.

I shrugged, "it wasn't me."

Still marveling at the very rare experience, the girls thundered back to shore, rattling the dock under their feet.

Melanie followed, reminding them to be careful and telling them that she had boiled some water and had hot washcloths in lieu of showers.

I paused a moment, turned to go, then glanced back up at the infinite tapestry of night.

Was it just me, or did the comet we had seen have a tinge of green?

Moyobamba, San Martin, Peru: two years earlier

I don't get motion sickness, but the bus driver must have been trying to win a bet and was giving me a run for my money.

The winding road from Tarapoto to Moyobamba led steadily upward through many a blind turn along the narrowest roadway I had ever seen. One and a half lanes at best, but this was a wide bus and the driver feared neither man nor car.

Fortunately, we were going uphill so Mad Max at the wheel couldn't coax maximum speed out of the behemoth, but he still seemed determined to cut down our two-and-a-half-hour drive time.

I was the only white onboard and as such had been charged a premium on the fare. Elder Geronimo, my Guatemalan companion, was sound asleep next to me. As was everyone else on the bus that I could see, otherwise I would have tried to share the Gospel with some other passengers.

I had a window seat which did nothing to assuage my fears that we were bound for a fall and a fiery crash.

Maybe the ever-present danger of careening off a cliff would get people thinking more about the hereafter and I could share a message about Heaven. Time went by and still everyone else seemed asleep as well or maybe they just didn't want to see the rollercoaster ride taking place out the windows and kept their eyes tightly closed.

I was proficient in Spanish and confident in my calling as a missionary for the Church of Jesus Christ of Latter-day Saints, but this was a new area for both Geronimo and me, and my first assignment as District Leader.

The remoteness struck me even more than that of my previous area, Iquitos, which was accessible only by plane and boat, but had a population ten times that of Moyobamba.

I rested my head against the window, seeing the rock face of the cliff just inches away on one side, and the valleys far below on the other.

I thought of the Apostle Paul's shipwreck, and figured that should we crash, it would be an equally good missionary opportunity at best, and at worst, well, at worst, I would die with Jesus Christ's name on the badge pinned to my breast pocket.

Not a bad way to go.

Even with our driver's Hollywood stunt tactics, we survived and disembarked just as the sun was setting over the mountains. I was tempted to kiss the ground now that we were back on *terra firma* and vowed to spend the rest of my missionary service in Moyobamba, and felt to say as Ammon did, that I would like to stay here perhaps until the day that I die. Because there was no way I was getting back on a bus headed downhill from here.

All the green reminded me of home. I had spent my first year in Peru along the coastal desert that was Lima, and the sweltering jungle of Iquitos, but this part of the country was different. The mountains, the low, fast-moving clouds, and the trees, albeit of a different variety, made me think of the Pacific Northwest.

I had that odd empty sort of homesick feeling that I only ever felt at twilight. Perhaps it was the transitional period when the world wasn't sure if it wanted to be day or night. It was like hangtime. What goes up, must come down, but there is always that brief moment when you're no longer rising, but haven't yet begun to fall.

Geronimo and I had served in the same district during the previous transfer and had become fast friends. I had predicted that we would one day be companions but had not expected it to happen so soon.

I was known as the smiling Elder, Elder *Sonrisa,* but he was even more gregarious than I was. He always had a joke or a story to tell and was endlessly optimistic.

As night fell in the town square, we found ourselves alone. It was cool and quiet. All the other passengers had dispersed and there was very little activity on the streets. We were unsure of where to go and began trying to find our accommodations by dead reckoning.

We found a dirt road that led out of the town. Streetlights were few and far between, making it hard to see the numbers scrawled on the gates of the houses and hovels we passed.

Geronimo and I spoke for the first little while but soon grew quiet the longer it took.

"Are you sure you have the right address?" He asked me.

I pulled the slip of paper out of my pocket and looked at it for what seemed like the hundredth time.

"Yep."

We kept going.

I thought I heard footsteps behind us, but each time we paused, so did the footsteps.

Geronimo also seemed to have noticed and we exchanged a look.

We set off again, trying to make our stops more random to try and catch our pursuer, if there was one, unawares. But it seemed like only an echo.

Except we were walking on soft earth, no chance of an audible reverberation.

"Let's just ask them for directions." I said.

"Why doesn't he just walk on by?" Geronimo asked.

"Maybe he knows we're missionaries and doesn't want us to preach at him."

"How would he know that?"

"Who else wears white shirts and ties and travels in pairs?"

We decided to walk a little further, then turn and start back the other way to try and meet the other person head on.

After several more steps we turned and stopped.

He was right behind us.

CHAPTER TWO

To awaken is to arise. I never understood the idea behind the snooze button. From the moment my eyes opened I was already moving towards my tent door.

Everyone else had slept in the cabins, Melanie and the Ayres in the east one and the girls had split between the north and west ones.

I could have slept inside the main building but that would not have been true camping.

The sun was barely peeking through the trees, and the embers of our fire from the night before still smoked ever so slightly in the breeze.

Breathing deep, I stretched and shook strength and feeling back into my limbs.

Even though I had scouted the campground the previous evening, I wanted to get the lay of the land in a different kind of light. Things can look dissimilar in the morning than they do at night, or even midday.

The sentinel pines of all varieties marched on in uneven rows as far as I could see. The beams of sunlight refracted off the motes of dust, dancing like an all-natural lava lamp. High in the trees, birds were already atwitter. The forest floor was dotted with rock and in some spots loamy and soft with a thick bed of pine needles, interrupted here and there with a deadfall or shed limbs.

I checked the flag and found it still right side up.

I saw lights from the main building and made my way to the kitchens. Sister Ayres and Melanie were already baking fresh scones with real butter and homemade jams. I knew that there was a wide-ranging debate as to whether scones were baked or fried. The jury was still out, and I didn't really care either way as long as there was some to eat.

"You missed dinner." Sister Ayres said, disapproving but gentle. I half expected her to lick her thumb and wipe something off my face, like I was an unruly child.

I smiled, quoting Charles Dickens. "'Subdue your appetite and you've conquered human nature'. If I had laid eyes on your meal, there would have been nothing left for anyone else."

Sister Ayres handed me a buttered scone.

"Thank you. I hate to eat and run but I have some activities to prepare for the girls."

Melanie pulled another tray of scones from the ovens. "Make sure you don't keep them busy all day, they wanted to do Jedi braids."

"What's that?" I asked.

She shrugged. "A hairstyle thing, I guess."

I bit the scone and made a chef's kiss gesture. "Sublime."

Wanting more scones but figuring I had to earn them, I took a quick detour to scrub some dishes in the stainless-steel sink. Then, with a scone in each hand, I headed for the woods.

"After breakfast would you send the girls out to the spot near where we had the fire last night?" I called to Melanie.

She smiled and winked and kept baking.

Back among the trees, I had scouted out a small clearing yesterday where the ground was mostly level and a little more hard-packed. A few large boulders lay scattered around as well as some smaller rocks. Picking the stones out of the way, I hid four slips of paper throughout the grove.

Then I lay back on the ground, lacing my fingers behind my head and closed my eyes. I heard the breeze moving through the treetops, the creak of boughs, twigs and cones hitting the forest floor like unsteady footfalls.

People sometimes think that you can find silence in nature but having spent as much time as possible outdoors, I hadn't ever found absolute quiet.

Peace, yes. But not utter silence.

Natural noise can be good and grounding, not like the grating grind of densely populated areas and wireless headphones.

God filled this world with sound, and you get to craft your own playlist that you can listen to on the best high-fidelity system in the world: your own head and your own heart.

In big cities they talk about light pollution and noise pollution and just plain regular pollution. Out here though, even with all the sounds it was the opposite of pollution. Which would be purification.

Noise purification.

I breathed deeply.

Air purification.

The sun scattered through the canopy.

Light purification.

I could have fallen asleep again right there in the middle of the morning. As a missionary one of my favorite companions, Elder Sanchez, was from Costa Rica, and there they have a saying, *pura vida.*

Pure life.

That's what it felt like right then.

You don't even have to go to the back of beyond to get a bit of a reset. Just spending time in a park, or backyard, just kindling your own fire, or being off social media for a week will do wonders. I sighed, patting my pockets, checking their contents. I thought about my past, present, and future. How marvelous is it that to God all things are present. The trees sighed in the breeze, and I wanted this moment to last forever.

A squirrel chittered away in some tree. Somewhere a bird of prey called.

They say that before you die your life flashes before your eyes. I didn't think I was at the point of death nor did I see memories strobing in my mind's eye. Rather, I felt as though I were flipping through a large faux-leather photo album of the amazing things that I had seen. Many of the plastic sleeves held no photographs behind them, yet.

I heard the girls laughing and chatting the way only teenagers can. I thought I felt the tremors in the earth as they approached. Like a stampede of wild horses.

I climbed up out of my reverie like a bear waking from hibernation.

Dusting myself off, I stood and smiled as the girls appeared, all bright-eyed and looking expectantly at me.

"What did you want us for, Brother Sawyer?" Aubrey asked.

I clapped my hands together. "It's time for some exercise."

My pronouncement was met with a collective groan.

I patted the air with my hands, "alright, alright, settle down. Not *that* kind of exercise— brain builders, just a couple of riddles. But first you have to find them. There are four pieces of paper each with a puzzle on them. Start looking."

They started scrounging around, turning over stones and leaves. People have a tendency to look low down when searching and neglect the space above them.

But they surprised me.

Kami found one of the clues tacked high up on the trunk of a tree. Emeline, Olivia, and Samantha each found one of the hidden papers and they took turns reading aloud.

"I look like an 'S' and sound like one, too."

"I sleep by my feet and hear what I see."

"My home is invisible, made by many limbs."

"Together I am not quite Omega, on my own I am not quite alone."

I smiled. "Okay, now it *is* time for some real exercise." I dropped down and started performing push-ups. "Alright, push-ups until someone can make a guess."

They all dropped down, some on their knees and began doing the best push-ups that they could.

I was impressed.

Suddenly Aubrey popped up. "Wait! Looks and sounds like an 's', that's gotta be a snake."

"Good job, Aubrey. Any other guesses for the rest of the riddles?"

No response.

"Okay, more push-ups."

After a minute Kaytee raised her hand. "Bats hang upside down to sleep and see with echo location."

"Perfect." I could tell that they were getting tired from the push-ups. "That's enough, everyone up."

They dusted off their hands and Ashlin hazarded a guess. "Octopi have lots of legs and can camouflage."

Samantha countered, "ants have six legs, and you can't see them underground."

"What if it means like limbs on a tree?" Taylor said.

Olivia ran the back of her hand across her brow and said, "It's a spider, duh. Their webs are practically invisible. Haven't you ever walked into one?"

We all shared a laugh.

"So, what about the last one?" I asked. They passed the paper around and read it to themselves.

"Look closely at the words."

Samantha drummed her fingers on her chin contemplatively, repeating the riddle slowly to herself, her lips moving silently.

Then she snapped her fingers, "Wolf!"

I nodded approvingly and gave her two thumbs up.

The girls cheered and asked her how she had come to the conclusion. "Easy, really." She said, "Omega made me think of Alpha. You know, like, the Lord is the *Alpha and Omega,* but also like an Alpha dog, or wolf in this case, the leader is called Alpha. Wolves together form a pack and a wolf by itself is called a lone wolf. Not quite *alone* because there is a space between *a* and *lone.*"

Emeline turned to me. "Are we done with exercises yet?"

"Almost. Let's run around the lake."

They were not overly enthusiastic about the prospect of a long run but after the first hundred yards they found a zeal, each vying for the lead position. Maybe the idea of an Alpha wolf resonated with them. They were young and spry, hurdling over obstacles and having a wonderful time.

The circumference was several miles long and eventually the girls began to slow down to a walking pace. The hike took hours, but the girls didn't seem to mind. They looked for birds or small forest animals and compared different rocks, trying to find arrowheads.

I didn't know anything about braiding hair or making friendship bracelets but if it came to teaching physical education and land navigation, I could hold my own. I wanted them to have a bit of a different camp experience than most activities geared toward females. Not just a glorified slumber party.

Winded and slightly sweaty, the girls talked each other into going for a swim. Hurrying back to their cabins to change.

I told them I would meet them at the dock in five minutes. Returning to my own tent, I donned a pair of shorts.

I went to the edge of the dock and dove in. The water was ice cold but deeply refreshing. I swam as far as I could under water before breaking the surface. The girls were making their way out to the end of the dock, followed by Stanislav.

Quickly, I swam back and pulled myself up onto the jetty.

Stanislav turned his heavy-lidded eyes to me as I walked towards him.

"Help you?" I asked.

"I am trained lifeguard. Must be lifeguard if you are going to swim."

"I'm a lifeguard." I said. Which wasn't strictly true. I had plenty of first aid experience and earned a lifeguarding merit badge back in the Boy Scouts. I figured that competitive swimming in high school had to count for something, though.

"Two is better than one, no?"

I didn't like the way he was eyeing the girls. All their bathing attire was modest, but they could have been in burqas and Stanislav's leering would have been just as offensive.

"Don't you have things to be taking care of? I mean, that is your job, isn't it?"

He sucked his teeth and regarded me with a different sort of appraisal. He had looked at the young women like a butcher gauges cuts of meat. He now eyed me the way a cobra watches a mongoose.

"This is my dock." He said softly but with a touch of menace. Just a hint, like a spice in a dish that you can't quite name, but you still taste it just the same.

I leaned forward, a familiar coolness that had nothing to do with the lake water sprang from deep in my soul and spread from my head to my toes. It was a calm, collected cold that rippled in my veins and curled my hands into fists.

"And these are my girls." I whispered back.

He nodded slowly, backed off the pier and disappeared back into the woods.

I breathed out.

I watched him go and tried not to let the girls see my rising anger, or my sense of worry.

There had been potential violence that had stalked the waters, and I didn't want it to ruin the mood.

I turned to face the girls, who looked proud and stalwart. Not like shrinking violets.

Running a hand through my wet hair, I said in as serious a tone as I could, "I don't want any of you to go anywhere alone, you got it?"

They nodded.

"Okay, last one in the water does all the dishes."

The splash was tremendous, and I couldn't have said who was the last in. It was probably me.

That night we sang songs around a roaring fire. We made tinfoil dinners and desserts. Brother Ayres played the guitar and sang. Melanie performed a skit with Sister Ayres and a couple of the girls did a comedy routine that had us all in stitches.

Eventually everyone got tired. Tasty food, wholesome fun, and lots of fresh air had left all of us ready for bed. None of the teenagers seemed to be concerned about their social media accounts. Their MyFace and Snapbook and Instachats all but forgotten out in the wild.

We said a prayer together and everyone wandered back to their bunks.

I had told Melanie at lunchtime about the confrontation between the caretaker and me. At first, she had seemed ready to scold me for my impetuosity. I endeavored to explain that it was one of my better qualities. She softened and thanked me for being so attentive.

Melanie had decided that she needed to show him her badge tomorrow and encourage him to avoid our group.

She and I stayed by the fire for a little while until she had to get up to check that the girls were settled in their beds.

Poking absently at the coals, I looked around the camp. There had been no sign of Stanislav since our encounter at the lake. Either he was a good caretaker in that he had decided to do all his work discreetly, or the very worst in that he didn't want to work at all anymore.

"You okay, Sawyer?" Melanie asked, swinging her Maglite by her side as she returned from making her rounds.

I put my hands up in mock surrender. "No problems here, Officer, I wasn't causing any trouble, I promise."

Laughing, she sat down next to me, and I wrapped an arm around her shoulders.

"What's on your mind." She asked.

"I can't put my finger on it. It's just a feeling, like unease. Have you ever been motion sick?"

"No." She said.

"Me neither, but I imagine it is something like that. It's the weird sensation when you're sitting in a parking lot and the car next to you starts driving away and you think you're the one moving."

"Is it that guy?" She jerked her thumb in the direction of Stanislav's trailer.

"I don't like the looks of him, but he seems like just a run-of-the-mill greasy guy. Nothing out of the ordinary. It's unfortunate but not unusual for a guy to be a creep to that degree." I tossed the stick I had been stoking the fire with onto the embers. It flared briefly and began to burn.

Melanie said nothing but I could feel her almond eyes taking in my own thoughts. She didn't try and talk me out of my preoccupation, she just watched and waited for signs, and for that I was grateful.

She had the gift of silence. Which made everything she said all the more valuable.

I looked back at her, and she looked deeper back at me.

I got the impression, as I had so many times before, that she could read me like a picture book.

"What do you want to do?" She asked.

"I think I need to go on a walk. I'm going to patrol the perimeter, make sure nothing is amiss." I realized she had just done the same thing, but she didn't try to dissuade me.

"Okay, Sawyer."

As I stood, she grasped my hand and pulled me back. We kissed softly.

"I love you, Sawyer. Everything is going to be all right."

"I love you, too." And I knew she was right. Deep down I knew everything would be all right, in an eternal sense. But what about temporally? What about right now? Tomorrow? The next day?

Who could say?

As I moved away from the fire, I felt the warmth on my back and the coolness of the night washed over my face like the finest mist.

My night vision, hampered by the firelight, took some time to adjust.

I moved slowly through the woods. Stopping at random intervals. Closing my eyes and stretching my ears.

Listening.

Smelling.

Nothing.

No howls or roars. No snapping of twigs under the paw of a mighty predator. No hissing in the grass, no metallic sounds of weapons being readied.

No harbinger of danger. No portents of imminent peril.

Nothing but the faraway stars that seemed so close and the darkness of the forest that really was.

I walked by the lake, racking my brain for some clue, some warning or indicator of what was gnawing at me.

Nothing.

But inspiration had always come to me, and it had always come in time. So far, anyway.

I moved within sight of the trailer but there was no light or sound from within.

After a little while, I wandered back to the fire. It was now reduced to only a couple coals, glowing faintly orange. Melanie must have gone to bed. All the lights were off in the cabins. I didn't think that I should be too far away from everyone, so instead of going all the way back to my tent I just curled up on the ground next to the dying fire and fell asleep.

Moyobamba, San Martin, Peru: two years earlier

He was tall and lean. Not quite gaunt, but the way his clothes hung off him like on a bent wire hanger, he could have passed for a scarecrow.

Geronimo jumped backwards in surprise, and I took a step forward, not exactly aggressively, but energetically. Ready to shake hands or throw a punch, whichever proved necessary. He paused in his approach, perhaps taken aback at my sudden movement towards him. I tried to take in everything at a glance. A split-second threat assessment. Even though his clothes hung loosely on him, I couldn't see signs of concealed weapons. His shoes looked to be expensive Oxfords. Nice dress shoes, but I wasn't worried about getting kicked by them. If they had been steel-toed boots it would have been another story.

In one hand he held what looked like an orchid. He stuck his other hand out in front, as if to halt my approach or wave in greeting. His fingers were long and slender, like a concert pianist's. There were several other abnormalities about his appearance that were noteworthy, but what surprised me the most was the fact that he was white.

Very white. Pale.

His head was bulbous and bald except for a scraggly horseshoe of blonde hair that trailed down over his shoulders like creeping ivy dying on a graveyard wall.

I stopped.

He started to speak in a hoarse whisper. I couldn't understand him.

"Excuse me?"

He smiled. "I'm sorry to have startled you. I'm Brother Kucera."

We shook.

His grip was strong.

Which surprised me, for someone of so slight a frame.

My experience in Peru so far had shown a decided lack of interest in firm handshakes among the locals.

He handed me the potted orchid, smiling wryly. "We thought you might have been Sister missionaries."

I handed the flower to Geronimo, wanting to leave my hands unhampered, still unsure of this stranger in the night.

"We?" I asked.

"The Bishop. Bishop Salinas. He sent me to meet you."

"Oh."

"I'll show you to your house."

He walked past us without looking back to see if we were following him.

I looked at Geronimo and he returned my gaze. Simultaneously, we shrugged and set off behind the stranger.

We hadn't walked much further before we reached a small house. It reminded me a bit of Bag End from J.R.R. Tolkien's timeless work. There was a low gate with natural growth all around it. A set of flagstones led up to the small door. A pair of citrus trees flanked the path just beyond the gate.

"Welcome, Elders." Brother Kucera said in his strange accent.

Realizing we hadn't introduced ourselves properly, we quickly gave him our names and thanked him again.

I wanted to ask him his story but didn't want to seem rude. He might have had some very good and clandestine reason for being far from home. There were plenty of American and European expatriates in South America, but Moyobamba seemed even more remote. At least in Lima there were about as many amenities as you would find in the First World.

Before I could attempt to broach the subject, he pointed further down the dirt road in a manner that reminded me of the Ghost of Christmas Future.

"The Chambi family next door will give you breakfast and the Bishop would like to meet with you in the morning."

With that, he set off again and was soon swallowed up by the darkness.

Geronimo pushed the door open and fumbled for the light switch. Several cockroaches beat a hasty retreat as the dull bulbs flickered on.

Geronimo set the orchid down on a wooden bench just inside the door and started searching for a shower.

We realized how tired we were and didn't even bother unpacking. After a quick rinse from the strangled and lukewarm stream, we found the knitted hammocks hanging in what passed for a bedroom and after a pair of sleepy prayers we rocked ourselves to sleep.

CHAPTER THREE

I enjoy dreaming. It is a unique experience, perfectly tailored to every individual and, only with exceedingly rare exceptions, different every time.

When I was a child, I used to wish I could record my dreams on VHS to watch them over and over again.

In my dream I awoke in an inferno akin to Dante's but there was no Virgil by my side. I realized with a sort of bemused detachment that I was still dreaming and decided that the setting for my nighttime vision was inspired by my proximity to the remains of the campfire.

Like Dante's ninth ring, the scene froze over, and I found myself at the edge of the lake, covered in ice. Testing the strength of the ice, I walked out a little way. My favorite dreams are the ones in which I can fly. I tried, getting a running start and leaping, but I could only briefly hover a foot off the ground.

Then a great shadow passed overhead, and a monstrous figure flew into view. It was the size of a truck with the body of a spider, the wings of a bat, the head of a wolf and the tail of a snake. As it reared to charge, the ice broke beneath its hairy appendages, and we were both plunged into the icy lake water.

It was dawn. I opened my eyes but did not startle or gasp awake like they do in the movies. Rolling over, I did a quick scan around, seeing nothing but a calm, midsummer morning. The smell of woodsmoke drifting in the air.

Then I saw Kaytee. She was hustling across the grounds towards Melanie's cabin. She looked upset but like she was keeping it together. That sort of almost-cry where no tears are shed but the bottom lip trembles ever so slightly. She held her arms across her chest, like she was staving off a severe chill. She was wearing an oversized hooded sweatshirt, and I could see a bright blush to her complexion.

"Kaytee, what's wrong?" I said, my voice too loud for the still morning.

She looked up, seeing me suddenly. There were tears forming in the corners of her eyes now and she dabbed at them with her sleeves.

Melanie's cabin door opened, and she came down the steps in her pajamas.

"Sawyer, you're going to wake up the kids—Kaytee? What's the matter, honey?"

Kaytee fell into her arms and whispered something to Melanie. I was too far away to hear it, but Melanie's olive complexion turned ashen. She looked at me, jerking her head towards the main building.

She was a good leader, a good cop. We had been together long enough that I understood her body language and I could infer enough from Kaytee. Something inside the building had very nearly hurt her.

Something bad.

I had never seen Melanie's eyes that fiery. Like molten iron ore.

Pushing the big door open with a creak, I scanned the interior. It was quiet and apparently deserted. There was a cast iron stove to heat the place in winter and a polished cement floor.

The kitchen was clean and empty.

The women's lavatory door stood ajar, and its fluorescent light was still activated from the motion sensor.

Moving towards the bathroom, I strained my ears for sounds. Maybe another girl had relayed some disquieting news, or had there been some sort of gossip, some bullying? What did the kids call it these days? The *tea*?

I doubted that a disagreement could have arisen between some of the girls. They were all friends.

I didn't think there was anyone in there, but decorum necessitated a knock and an announcement.

"Hello?" I said, rapping my knuckles on the door jamb as I nudged the door itself open further.

Then I heard it, some scrabbling and rustling. In the air vent. A raccoon? A squirrel? The vent was large and square, set into the wall above head height. The mesh grating was not wide, but I could make out the shape of a head.

"Stalinislav?" I said.

"Yes, I realize there was no ventilation and try to fix before breakfast. I think I scare young lady. I come now."

At the far end of the bathroom, passed the stalls and showers, a door to the janitorial supply closet opened. Stanislav appeared, looking sheepish and sweaty. Too sweaty for the mild morning, even in the close quarters of the crawl space.

He held a cellphone in his hand.

"It fixed now. Sorry to disturb." He moved as if to go around me.

I am not what you would call non-confrontational. I don't just accept conflict. I embrace it.

Heartily.

I put my left hand on Stanislav's chest and was a little surprised to feel solid muscle beneath his work shirt. I shoved and even though he stepped back, it was not as far as I had intended to push him.

His features looked more like Rasputin now, especially his eyes, and when he spoke it was no longer like the deferential foreigner with a can-do attitude.

It was pure poison.

"You set finger again on me, I keep your hand."

I kind of raised my hackle, like a snarling pit bull, and said, "cellphones don't work up here, at least not for calls. So what are you doing with that?"

He blinked and looked down at the mobile device in his hands as though he had just noticed it for the first time.

"I save instructions in phone. Take picture of book." He made a swiping, dismissive gesture, "It nothing."

"Let me see it, Stalingrad." I said, reaching a hand for the phone.

He said nothing, but the poison had spread from his voice to his eyes and before I knew it, he had thrown the phone at my head. Turning to avoid the projectile, I left myself vulnerable as Stanislav charged into me, knocking me back against the row of sinks. Bouncing off the porcelain with a grunt, I brought my elbows in and raised my fists. He was ready for me and as I straightened up from the sink, he caught me with a right to the jaw that started me spinning around like I had been caught in a whirlpool.

Using the considerable force of his blow, I let myself turn a full circle, but I ducked down as I turned and twisted, like a compressed spring. He was expecting to turn me, but he wasn't ready for my crouch. He stepped in with a scything right elbow that cut the air right where my head should have been.

His missed strike carried him forward and off balance, his boot squeaking on the tile. His right side was perfectly exposed, and I smashed a digging left uppercut to his kidney that must have registered on all the seismographs.

Stanislav swore and tried with the same elbow, this time reversed and aimed downwards. I couldn't dodge it, so I turned and took the attack on the meat of the upper arm.

It stung but didn't debilitate me. I was moving fast and managed to get behind him, wrapping my arms around his waist. He was taller and heavier than me, but I still lifted him off the ground.

Most wrestlers are accustomed to being thrown, it's part of the deal, happens to everyone at one time or another. They are ready for it, trained for it. So, when I picked up Stanislav, I felt him try to shift his weight, preparing for the slam, thinking about how to land and brace for the fall.

But it never came.

I just lifted him, and I squeezed.

Crushed him to me.

Like a garbage compactor.

Just as he began to panic, I heard popping from either his ribs or spine.

Better than a chiropractor.

He clawed at my arms and hands, kicked backwards with heels. He was heavy and strong, and I was losing my grip when he managed to get his foot against a sink, and pushed off hard, sending us crashing backwards.

Smashing against the wall, my grip slackened. Stanislav wasted no time stepping away but leaping back with another right elbow. Barely slipping out of the path of the oncoming strike in time, his blow shattered several tiles and broke through the wall. He must have hit a pipe or a stud or conduit or something because he howled in pain, baring his teeth and grabbing at his arm with his free hand.

Which was all the invitation I needed. I skipped forward and butted him in the face with my forehead. As he rocked back from the blow, I clipped him on the chin with a short left hook, followed by my own right elbow, thrown high and wide.

It split the meat above his left eyebrow, showering blood across the broken tile in raindrop patterns.

He was a scumbag, but a tough one. Any single one of my hits would have knocked down most opponents. He stayed standing though, only stumbling against the wall. Pushing off, he swung a spinning back fist that missed, but I had given him too much room. I was expecting, hoping for more action. This was my kind of fighting, the knock-down, drag-out, blood and vinegar, no-holds-barred, barroom brawling kind. I had his number and was sure that the next exchange would have him picking up his teeth with broken fingers.

But he wasn't having it.

He ran.

Our relative positions had changed, leaving him closer to the door.

Well, darn.

Following at a run, I crashed through the front door just as it swung back shut from his flight.

I did not want him to secure to a vehicle, or to get a hostage, of which there were plenty of potential targets.

Melanie, the Ayres, and all the girls were standing outside in a tight semi-circle. As one body, they recoiled at the sight of Stanislav. More and more he was resembling a cornered animal, turning this way and that.

I breathed in, breathed out, slowing down, not wanting to chase him right into the bystanders.

"It's over, Sputnik, don't make it any worse." I said.

Melanie stepped forward, even without a badge and gun she still cut a commanding figure. "I'm a deputy with the San Diego County Sheriff's Office, and you are under arrest."

Stanislav started to run again, away from the camp and towards the woods. He vaulted a fallen tree and charged through undergrowth, sending up a spray of leaves and pine needles.

Melanie and I exchanged looks and I motioned with my chin towards the road. "Get ahold of the park ranger, I'll get the bad guy."

She called after me, but I didn't hear what she said, I was already running after the man who had threatened a young woman under my protection and there was no distance, no time, and no way that I wouldn't catch him.

CHAPTER FOUR

The trees were even more closely-knit to the northeast, which is the way he fled. The camp was quickly out of view and the morning sun became muted by the canopy.

Stanislav's trail was easy enough to follow, though. Chunks of loam were churned up where he had stepped. There were plenty of broken stems that showed white and fresh where he had passed through the underbrush.

I didn't think he would be able to maintain his breakneck pace through the woods for long. We were at altitude, he was a big guy, and the foliage grew increasingly dense.

But I still couldn't see him.

Slowing down, I strained my ears for any sound of him. *Nothing.*

Maybe he was holed up somewhere, hiding behind a tree with a branch or rock to try and brain me with.

I moved ahead at irregular intervals. Rushing forward, stopping, inching ahead, then running again with plenty of zigzagging.

If he was trying to mask the sound of his movement with mine, then he wouldn't be able to start and stop at the same time, or, alternatively, if he was planning an ambush, he wouldn't know when to time his attack. No pattern that he could follow.

Being unpredictable is not complicated but it isn't natural either.

And the erratic movements cost me more of my own energy.

I was no great tracker, and the evidence of his passing became less obvious when I came to a stonier patch of ground.

As unpredictable as I was trying to be, I realized Stanislav was more so. By definition, undetected criminals are not predictable because no one suspects them to be committing crimes.

It is a tricky tight rope to walk because giving too much freedom of action to the bad guys equates to a threat just as much as does cornering them. Too many and too few options always make them dangerous.

I couldn't imagine what his plan was, running off like that. Maybe he had another hideout—a cabin, or something. Maybe there were other trails, fire-access or logging roads or some such thing.

Then I got a sinking feeling in the pit of my stomach.

What if he had doubled back?

Chances were he knew these woods better than I did and it would have been no great feat to lead me away before creeping back to camp.

But no, Melanie could handle that. She hadn't brought her weapon, but she was as strong as any warrior-princess. And even I wouldn't want to tangle with Sister Ayres armed with a rolling pin or kitchen knife.

I considered calling out, trying to get Stanislav to surrender and "come quietly", but I hesitated. Maybe he hadn't even realized yet that I was in pursuit.

Squatting down like the Indian scouts in the movies, I looked for any sign on the ground of his passing.

Nothing.

Straightening up, I whirled around at a sound in the underbrush. It was coming from behind, some ways off but approaching.

Maybe he had doubled back after all, not back to camp, but to get behind me.

The sound stopped.

An animal?

Then I heard rustling ahead of me.

Did Stanislav have a whole contingent of comrades ready to surround me? Or had I just stumbled upon a group of deer?

I moved on, trying to split my attention both behind and before me.

The way ahead sloped up before dropping back down into a circular depression, kind of like a funnel full of trees.

I almost lost my footing moving on the decline, catching myself against the base of a pine.

I saw churned-up earth at the bottom of the slope. Moving closer, I glimpsed the stark contrast of synthetic clothing against the natural background, partially concealed by a huge deadfall. Looking from the work shirt and canvas pants to a pair of boots, toes up and heels dug in. It reminded me of the scene in the Wizard of Oz when Dorothy's house drops on the Wicked Witch of the East and her ruby-slippered feet protrude from under the abode.

I figured he had fallen, hit his head and knocked himself out cold before I could.

An all-too-perfect scenario.

As the rest of him came into view, I saw that the nature of his incapacitation was much more permanent.

Stanislav lay on his back, but his neck was twisted at an unnatural angle that not even the best yogi or contortionist could mimic.

I moved closer to him. He wasn't the first dead guy I had seen and wouldn't be the last.

It seemed unlikely that a simple slip could have resulted in a broken neck, but stranger things had happened.

Then I heard movement behind and above me. Someone, or something, was coming up behind me.

Diving behind a tree, I waited with bated breath.

Perhaps a bear or another carnivore was coming for an easy meal.

I heard labored breathing from someone moving fast, a yelp, and the unmistakable sound of someone falling.

I stepped back out from behind my cover in time to see a tangle of limbs, both human and arboreal.

Kami, armed with a stout tree bough, rolled end over end. I moved to help her up.

"Brother Sawyer!" She exclaimed breathlessly, pine needles in her hair but looking none the worse for wear.

"What are you doing here?"

"I just thought you might need some help. I know Aikido."

"I don't need any help." I said.

She looked perturbed and more than a little miffed. "Well, he got away from you the first time, so you definitely do."

I shook my head, "No, no, sorry Kami, I meant I don't need help *anymore*. He's dead."

Mouth agape, she took a step backwards. "Dead? Did—did you kill him?"

"Me? No. He took a tumble too, but it looks like he broke his neck."

Kami was made of stern stuff. I had seen her in action at a couple of youth group activities that Melanie and I had supervised. I had seen her throw tomahawks at a Pioneer Day celebration, outrun most boys and I had even taught her some boxing to supplement her other martial arts prowess.

Had it been any of the other kids, I wouldn't have been so blunt about the situation.

Of which even I didn't have a firm grasp of yet anyway.

I ran my hand contemplatively across my chin.

Kami said, "We can't just leave him here. Animals will get to him."

I looked at her. "You mean you want to carry him back with us?"

"No, just bury him."

I could see her trying not to be sick. Tough though she was, a dead body wasn't something you just got comfortable with.

"Kami, he was a bad, dangerous guy. He can't hurt anyone now. We don't have a shovel and even if we did, I wouldn't break a sweat for this creep. If the critters get him, so be it. I am going to check his pockets though, how about you go back up the hill and keep watch? I bet Melanie has everyone out searching for you by now."

She nodded and scurried back up the slope.

Patting down his pockets, I found very little of interest. No weapons, no wallet, and no phone since he had thrown it at me during our fight. I did find a bit of paper with what looked like a foreign phone number scrawled on it. I pocketed it just in case.

Stanislav had been a big guy in life. In death, he looked deflated. Like merely a husk. I wasn't sad about his demise, but it was a shame that he had been so unprepared to meet his Maker.

"Sawyer!"

Kami was doing the whisper-shout thing and gesticulating wildly. Wiping my hands on my jeans, I ran up the slope next to her.

"There." She whispered hoarsely.

I looked where she was pointing, saw nothing. Then I caught a glimpse, just barely. Something between the trees, a large figure, loping along at a decent clip.

Not a person.

An animal.

"What is it?" Kami asked.

I just shook my head in disbelief. It didn't move in the slinking manner of a mountain lion, and it wasn't large enough to be a bear. Wrong color, too. This creature was white.

"A wolf." I said.

"There are still wolves in California?"

I shook my head again. "Not really, only one confirmed family. There was another that disappeared a few years ago."

"What do we do?" Kami asked.

"Looks like a lone wolf. No big deal, but let's get hurry up and get back to camp, okay?"

Kami nodded and we wound our way back through the trees, angling away from the wolf's evident route. There was a slight breeze that remained favorable, keeping us downwind.

But the breeze also brought a dense layer of fog that turned the forest into an almost unrecognizable alien landscape.

The wolf would blend into the mist like a ghost if it were hunting us, and we were not even able to see more than three trees in

It got dark quickly.

We didn't speak until we realized we were lost.

It had been very early morning when I had confronted Stanislav, but the pursuit had taken us much further than I had imagined.   In my attempts to keep us away from the wolf, we had veered too far off course. We only knew our bearing was off when we almost stepped into the lake.

"Are we lost?" Kami asked.

"No, not anymore, we just follow the lake until we get to camp. Either way around will lead us home."

Eventually the fog began to lift, and the higher clouds were hurrying across the sky.

The first stars were coming out.

We opted to stay on the shore, it would take longer following the curves of the lakefront but even a short way into the woods and we would have been in deeper darkness.

We hadn't seen the wolf again.

As the wind died down, the lake was rendered as still as glass except for the occasional splash and ripples of feeding fish. The miniature waves made the reflected stars dance and shimmer.

It was a moonless night but far away above the trees I caught a faint orange glow.

Melanie must have started a bonfire.

I thought it strange that we didn't hear anyone out looking for us, especially as we got closer to camp. No shouts, no dancing flashlight beams through the trees. Maybe Melanie figured that Kami would be safe with me. But how would she have known that Kami hadn't gotten lost, or worse? For all they knew Stanislav was still loose in the forest.

Which made some kind of sense that they had all stayed in a group if they thought I hadn't apprehended him yet.

I suddenly got a bad feeling that emanated from the pit of my stomach all the way out through the top of my head and the tips of my fingers. Not a cold, creeping dread, but the sudden, burning sensation—the realization that something is wrong.

My heart skipped a beat.

"Come on." I said to Kami and started running.

CHAPTER FIVE

My right foot sank into a muddy, soupy spot along the lake. My momentum almost made me fall but I managed to pull free, staggered, and resumed my run.

I heard Kami pounding along behind me, keeping pace, not asking questions.

We rounded a finger of land that jutted out into the water, and skirted around a fallen tree that was partially submerged in the lake with its root base on the shore.

Then we saw the camp.

Everything looked normal.

Melanie sitting next to an immense crackling bonfire with Kaytee, Aubrey, Olivia, Emeline, Samantha, Ashlin, Taylor, and Caeli.

Kami began to continue forward but I put an arm out, holding a finger to my lips.

We were still positioned well back in the trees along the lakeshore, invisible to the group around the firelight.

She gave me a weird look as I motioned her backwards and away from the campsite. She did the whole teenage thing of knitting her eyebrows together and raising her arms and opening her mouth slightly as if to say *what the heck?*

But to her credit she did not protest verbally and instead followed me further back into the dark, perhaps thinking I meant to play an untimely prank on the rest of the group.

"What's going on?" She whispered exasperatedly.

"Did you notice anything weird back there?"

"Yes! You! You're acting weird."

I couldn't help but smile, "I'm always weird, Kami. But we've got a problem. Did you notice they weren't singing, or roasting marshmallows, or talking?"

"Uh, yeah, they are probably worried sick about us. We've been gone all day."

I shook my head. "When did you ever know Aubrey and Olivia to not lead everyone in song and prayer? Especially if they were worried about us. And where are the Ayres?"

"Asleep? They're old."

"No, something is very wrong. They wouldn't rest if they were worried. I think there's trouble and the last thing we are going to do is wander into the middle of a trap."

"A trap?" She asked.

I nodded. "Everyone else is the bait. The bonfire is too big, and they are too quiet."

"If it's a trap, then who set it?"

I glanced back at the camp. "I don't know, maybe some of Stanislav's comrades."

"What are we going to do?" She asked.

I squatted on my heels, pursed my lips. "They set a trap; we're going to set our own."

I rehearsed my plan to her, and she added some of her own embellishments. We took up our positions. She went back towards camp, and I situated myself in a good vantage point.

She counted two minutes in her head and then made all sorts of noise, running towards the fire.

"Sister Clark! Sister Clark! Come quick, Sawyer's hurt, he tripped on a root I think and hit his head, he's not moving!"

Everyone looked up from the fire and I caught movement from behind both the main building and the Ayres' cabin.

Two figures, dressed in dark shirts and pants and carrying serious-looking rifles. The men were short, with shaved heads, and dark eyes. One was fat and one was lean. Both had

Musketeer mustaches. Something about them was vaguely familiar, but I couldn't place them in the semi-darkness and with crazy shadows from the dancing flames moving across the scene.

I could see Kami stiffen in surprise, but she continued the ruse.

"Please, someone, I can't move him, you need to help."

The fat one slapped Kami a ringing blow. Melanie was on her feet, but the lean one jabbed her in the back with the barrel of his rifle, knocking her off balance.

A bad mistake. Getting too close to Melanie.

She stumbled, then whirled around, grabbing for the rifle. The lean guy reeled back, nearly tripping.

Melanie lunged forward, like a lioness onto a gazelle.

Then the night was ripped by gunfire. Melanie skidded to a halt. The fat one had his rifle aimed in the air. He leveled it, not at Melanie but at Kami, then each of the other girls in turn.

"Don't even think about it, *chica.* "

Involuntarily, I started forward, then stopped. They had undoubtedly been waiting for me to stroll into camp. I needed them to come into the dark. To come looking for me. It was the only way to mitigate the potential for collateral damage.

Kami could handle herself, and if she and Melanie could have acted simultaneously, they might have gained the upper hand. But the moment passed, and both men moved out of arm's reach.

Kami, still holding her cheek from the slap, made a half-hearted attempt to continue the story she and I had concocted, but the fat one made a hissing noise to shush her and lifted his hand threateningly.

As far as I was concerned, his grave just got six feet deeper.

"Sawyer! We know you are out there, *amigo*. Come here or we start burning their hands. We need them mostly unharmed, but their extremities are expendable."

I didn't move.

They had given me invaluable information about their intentions.

They wanted the girls, unharmed.

And now I remembered them.

The previous autumn, Melanie and I had gone to Mexico chasing a false lead on the whereabouts of some other teenagers and had been waylaid by associates of these two banditos.

I had been caught flat-footed back then, but Melanie had disarmed and shot them both, saving us and a Mexican hardware store owner.

I remembered speculating then on the likelihood of their survival. Melanie had not shot to kill, only to wound, which can be a tall order even for someone with good accuracy. You never know what a bullet will do, exactly. There are all kinds of arteries and bullets can bounce off bone and go any which way.

But these guys had survived.

Now here they were.

Improbable as it seemed, the old nightmare had found us in the back of beyond. The girls all had tears welling in their eyes but must have been ordered into silence because they didn't make a peep.

The fat one paused another beat, then jerked his head at the lean one.

"Soto, burn one." He said in Spanish. They must have known that I understood their language.

Soto kept his rifle pointed at Melanie and moved around behind the girls, then he grabbed Aubrey by her platinum blonde hair and jerked her towards the fire.

I gritted my teeth, I had to do something. Melanie had beaten them before and we could beat them again now, but how?

The fat one called out again, "last chance, Sawyer. Or else we roast her pretty hand."

My fingers closed over a baseball sized rock. I could throw pretty accurately, but I couldn't count on beaning Soto hard enough to kill or concuss him, especially with him having human shield. My father had played ball in college, a shortstop, and a pitcher, but I had only ever favored pugilistic pastimes. Instead, I found another, similarly sized stone, and readied it in my left hand.

Then I threw the first rock, aiming it for the other side of the camp, hoping it didn't hit one of the cabin roofs.

Everyone turned at the soft sound it made.

I swapped my second rock to my right hand and threw it in the same direction, but not quite as far. It landed in the dark, but closer to them.

I figured that to them it might sound like approaching footsteps. Their backs were to me. I was only thirty yards away. I rehearsed my movements, hit the fat guy first, a crushing elbow to the base of his skull. Take his rifle and shoot the lean one named Soto.

I had never killed anyone before. I'm generally a peace-loving man, and as bad as they were, I really didn't want to kill them, but I wasn't exactly being overwhelmed with options.

I steeled myself, crouched, and went to move.

And stopped.

I felt the razor edge of a blade against the nape of my neck.

CHAPTER SIX

I didn't move. I didn't even breathe. Then a powerful hand the size of a catcher's mitt closed around my throat, and I was straightened up and flung bodily forward. I hit the dirt hard, rolled around to face my assailant, trying to get up but was hit in the chest with what felt like a freight train.

I fell back and just lay there. I was within the light of the fire now, and I heard some muted gasps and cries of concern.

Looking up, trying to regain the wind that had been knocked out of me, I saw my attacker emerge like Bigfoot from the woods and the shadows. He had to have been seven feet tall, with a chest like a vending machine and arms more knotted than the trees that surrounded us.

His face, like carved mahogany, was impassive. A noble, Aztec-looking face, with a wide brow and prominent nose. His mouth was closed and curved downward but his eyes, impossibly dark, seemed to absorb the light of the fire like a black hole and send it back like twin visions of hell.

In one hand he held a Sayoc tomahawk, the other fingered a talisman slung around his neck. Both items looked comically small, like children's toys, in his massive paws.

The giant took another long stride forward, raising the tomahawk and I knew that I was going to die.

Time stood still, and it was like I could see everything from a bird's eye view. For all my twists and turns, all my schemes and stratagems, all my calculations and cunning that I had developed over a lifetime of trouble, I could see no way out of this one.

I thought about my family, about Melanie, the Ayres, the girls, everyone I had ever known and loved and prayed that they would be all right without me.

Better off, maybe.

Contrary to common belief, your life doesn't flash before your eyes. It turns, like a merry-go-round, or the pages in a book where you've sketched a series of images in the corner, that when flipped quickly, appear to move in their own animation.

I caught still-life snapshots, glimpses of people and faraway places. Absurdly, I remembered the poem by Dylan Thomas about not going gently into death. I knew that we all had to go sometime, and I wasn't planning on putting up too much of a fuss when my time came. All I was worried about was getting to Heaven.

But, given the fact that I was leaving the woman I loved and the girls for whom I was responsible in dire circumstances, I figured a little rage was in order.

If I was going to die, something was going with me.

For all the giant's reach, I knew that I was out of range for him to strike me, so he would have to throw the tomahawk. I did not think I could dodge it in time, but if I could just move to my right take the hit on the left shoulder, I just might be able to retrieve the weapon with my strong hand. I would be badly wounded but, if I could move fast enough, I could cut down the fat one who was to my right. Take his gun and shoot the giant, hoping he wasn't bullet-proof.

Where was David and his sling when you needed him?

Soto, the lean one, would be the hardest. He still had Aubrey in his clutches and would likely get a shot off in the time it took me to deal with the other two. But I knew I only needed to even the odds for Melanie enough to give her a fighting chance.

I still couldn't catch my breath from the blow the behemoth had struck me, but I straightened up and felt the rough-hewn logs of one of the cabins behind me. I leaned back against the wall, bracing myself for what came next.

Time resumed, and the giant's arm kept coming up and back, then straightened forward, his fingers like summer sausages splayed out. I heard the fat one yell something like, "No, Tobar!" but I was waiting for the impact of cold steel, trying to sway and roll with it to lessen the damage, bringing up my right hand to snatch it out of the air if I could, or to extricate it from out of my body if I couldn't.

Too slow.

The wicked-looking tomahawk whistled by my ear, maybe even cutting a few stray hairs off. It hit the cabin with a dead, hollow sound, right next to my face.

I turned and looked at the polished surface and could see a wavy approximation of my reflection, like a funhouse mirror.

It was buried deep, and I knew that I never would have been able to pull it from the wood in time to execute my plan.

In Spanish, the fat guy reprimanded the giant. "Tobar, careful, you know we need him alive and unharmed. Unharmed, you understand."

The giant said nothing, just kept looking at me with an intensity hitherto unknown to me. I had faced a few bad guys in my time, but they had been systematic in their evil. I knew this was a chaotic force of nature.

No.

Not nature.

Nothing in the natural world could be so evil. Animals will hunt and fight and kill one another if they must, but they don't expend great efforts planning out cruel and unusual ways to make each other's lives miserable.

This guy was the antithesis to the natural order. He was an apex predator whose very life force seemed to be derived from his propensity to inflict pain and suffering. I was surprised that the fire didn't simply extinguish in the all-encompassing darkness of his presence.

I hadn't seen him for more than a minute, but I knew that I was looking at a demon. A soul-taker. On the handle of the tomahawk, I saw more than two dozen notches that I could only assume was his way of keeping count of his kills.

So why was he working for the little guys?

The giant walked over to me, face to face, or rather face to pectoral. He leaned down, braced one hand on the wall and pulled the tomahawk free with the other.

The talisman, hung on a strip of leather, dangled in front of me and I got a clear view of the thing.

It was white, made of bone or ivory, roughly worked but clearly carved in the likeness of a grinning devil with horns and fangs and claws.

The giant's skin glowed unnaturally in the firelight, and he grinned at me. It was all teeth and no heart.

I still hadn't breathed properly, and when he stepped away, I gasped audibly. Like I had been drowning.

I turned to the fat guy.

He shrugged and shook his head in a jocular fashion, as if to say, "*giants, am I right?*"

Then he said, "Mister Sawyer, please sit down with us."

He didn't tell me where, so I moved next to Melanie. Soto had released Aubrey and he held up a hand to stop me. He patted me down and took what few but important items I had in my pockets away from me. He put them in his own pocket and took up a position opposite the fat guy.

The giant produced a whet stone from a pouch on his belt and sat with his back to us at the very edge of the firelight. The slow, steady rasp of steel on stone punctuating every few words of the fat man's pronouncement. His English was good, but I would have rather he just spoke Spanish to me so that no one else could have understood.

"Mister Sawyer, you are, as I am sure you have surmised, in a lot of trouble. You and the lady cop caused many delays, many problems, for many powerful people."

He gestured towards himself and Soto. "As far as Soto and I are concerned, that is plenty of water under the bridge, no? But our employer wants blood for blood. What does your Bible-book say? An eye for an eye and a tooth for tooth? I think it is a matter of reputation. Some people can be very vain, very proud. But what that means is you will not be harmed, for now. The young women are safe, from us, at least. I am sure you can imagine what their destiny is. So, sleep. While you can. We have a long walk tomorrow."

I was so at a loss for words or action that I quietly acquiesced, my eyes rarely leaving the giant.

They ushered us into a single cabin and closed the door. I heard a chain rattle against the wood and the click of a padlock.

The tears were starting up again from some of the girls.

Melanie gently hushed them, and I motioned everyone to our knees.

We needed the power of prayer, not to mention several pairs of wings and maybe an entire armored division or a tactical nuclear strike.

But even just a prayer would suffice.

I prayed and then Melanie offered one of her own, followed by each of the girls in turn. It was a warm feeling that stole into my heart and, from what I could sense, into everyone else's as well.

The quiet sobs and sniffles subsided.

We must have prayed for more than thirty minutes. Then they all feel soundlessly asleep.

A tender mercy in the midst of a hurricane of fear.

But neither Melanie nor I thought of rest.

We had a lot to talk about.

"What happened?" I asked.

"When you went after that guy, the Ayres said they were going to go to the ranger's station. They are our best chance. I don't think these guys know about the Ayres. I am sure the rangers will be here be here at first light, if not before. They'll probably get someone from the Sheriff's as well. You had been gone awhile when we realized Kami was missing, too. We all guessed she was with you, but we were about to start searching when Soto and the other man, Lugo, I think he's called, showed up They just walked into camp, smiling and pointing their guns."

"They came in on foot?"

Melanie nodded.

"Did they have packs and gear? Did their boots look muddy or dusty?"

"Day packs, and the guns, we didn't hear any vehicles and there are no other driveable roads that would get them right to camp."

"Which direction did they come from?"

She thought about it for a second and then oriented herself from indoors. She pointed to the east.

"What about coms? Radios, cell phones?"

"I didn't see anything like that, but they burned all the girls' phones."

"What about the big one, Tobar?"

She shuddered. "He showed up not long before you and Kami got back. He gives me the creeps. He came and inspected all of us, smelled our hair. It was awful. Soto told us that he had been tracking you, that he had killed Stanislav."

My heart seized up again. I had been mere minutes away from the monster.

I nodded. "Kami and I found his body. His neck was broken, I thought it might have been an accident—a fall or something. I should have known that it was an attack. The wicked punish the wicked, I guess, but I still wouldn't have wished that on him."

"Did you find anything?" Melanie asked.

"On the body? Nothing of much interest. He threw his phone at me in the bathroom

Tobar must have followed Kami and me all the way back to camp and we never even heard a sound.

Closing my eyes, I tilted my head back, bouncing it gently off the wall, trying to knock some inspiration into my head, Sir Isaac Newton-style.

Melanie touched my cheek to snap me out of my brooding. "I know you're an empathetic guy, but I'm surprised you're this torn up about that janitor creep."

"It's not that. I don't care about him. I just can't believe I got out-foxed in the forest. That never happens. I'm no Jeremiah Johnson, but I'm an experienced woodsman and still I had no idea that Tobar was out there. I bet he wasn't more than a stone's throw away from Kami and me at any given moment. I'm sorry I left, I should have just stayed here and gotten you all out of Dodge."

"You didn't see anything else?"

"Well, Kami and I spotted a wolf, a white wolf."

"A wolf? All by itself? No way."

"Do you think Tobar is a werewolf?"

She just looked at me.

"I'm just saying." I smiled despite myself. Then I remembered where we were and what we were dealing with, and I hit the back of my head harder against the wall in frustration.

Melanie cupped both her hands around my face and pulled my gaze to hers.

"This isn't like you, Sawyer. Snap out of it. You never recriminate yourself or worry about why it went wrong. You can't change what happened, let's just fix it."

I knew she was right, but I couldn't stand the haunting, helpless feeling. I had been in precarious situations before. Melanie and I had defeated a group of human traffickers when we had first met but, like the many-headed hydra, it had sprouted back to bite us.

We sat in silence for a moment, then she whispered, "Maybe I should have just killed them back in Mexico."

I considered that. "No, Melanie, don't you go and agonize over the what ifs now, too. The what ifs will tear us to bits. We'll just have to hope that the Ayres don't walk into a trap as well. You're sure these jerks have no idea about the Ayres?"

"I don't see how they could know. They didn't come by from the road, they came through the woods, around the other side of the lake entirely, and well after the Ayres had left."

"I'm thinking that the phone number I found in Stanislav's pocket was a Mexican phone number. He must have been in cahoots with them and might have given them a sitrep with our numbers. But maybe not. He wasn't the sharpest bulb in the drawer."

She smiled slightly at my amalgamation of expressions.

"In the meantime, there are bears and cougars that would be happy to eat those guys for a midnight snack. Maybe they'll wander into camp for a little Mexican food."

She elbowed me in the ribs. "Quiet, the girls might hear you."

"In fact, that wolf that Kami and I saw, if it isn't Tobar's beast form, could come in handy. With any luck it will sneak into camp and go for their jugulars"

She tucked her dark hair behind her ears and snuggled in closer.

We were hostages, we had kids in our care who were now in grave danger, we were surrounded by evil men and had no idea what tomorrow would bring. But, on the grand scale of things, it was not a bad night. We were not restrained, we weren't injured, we likely had help on the way, and most important of all, God was with us.

I had been using up a lot of adrenaline all day long and my exhaustion was getting the better of me. I waited until Melanie fell asleep on my shoulder and then my eyes began to slowly close, like automatic blinds, or those projector screens in school you pull down in front of the whiteboard. My head nodded and my chin rested on my chest, and I fell asleep.

Moyobamba, San Martin, Peru: 2 years before
The next morning, after breakfast, Geronimo and I studied the scriptures and exercised together. There was not an abundance of workout equipment, but we did find some cinder blocks that we swung around like kettlebells, super-setting with pushups. I had also bought two pairs of boxing gloves, so we were able to spar.

It made for a very interesting companionship inventory when we knew we were going to be able to punch each other at some point.

Afterwards, we went to introduce ourselves to the Church leadership.

Bishop Salinas was happy to see us but expressed some concern in the apparent lull in effective missionary work. There had been plenty of visitors on Sundays but after only a couple lessons with the previous missionaries, they had stopped attending.

"What about the members?" I asked. "Have they been able to introduce friends and family to the missionaries?"

"It's a small congregation." Bishop Salinas said. "Small, but strong. Unfortunately, they are lacking a bit of confidence in the missionaries. Honestly, we were hoping for Sisters instead of Elders. They just seem to work better."

I smiled, unoffended because, in some cases, he was right.

"That's why Brother Kucera brought us an orchid." Geronimo said. "He thought we were going to be *Hermanas.*"

The Bishop appeared to backtrack, "we are glad you're here, of course, it is just going to be a bit of an uphill battle, but I can see that you two get along and a united companionship is half the battle."

"Three quarters." I said. "Jesus Christ said if ye are not one ye are not mine."

"It looks like we have our work cut out for us." Geronimo said. "Anyone you want us to visit first?"

"As a matter of fact, yes. His name is Brother Anibal."

"Where can we find him?" I asked.

The Bishop ran a hand over the top of his head and sighed. "Prison."

I have never been able to dictate the course of my dreams, but I can always recall them in detail. They have proved prophetic in the past and even though a lot of dreams can be discounted as the result of diet or just the dregs of an overactive imagination coupled with healthy doses of either good or bad memories, there is definitely something to them.

If dreams were meaningless then God would not have given us the ability to dream.

The scriptures have several instances of dreams as revelations. I had read a book, a manual really, called "Enter the Dream Realm" by Chris Hardman. It was insightful.

This night, all I could see was darkness.

Darkness and, a long way off, something else.

A looming figure bathed in spectral light. The illumination and the distance were such that, while I could see the figure moving, I wasn't sure if it was coming closer or retreating from me.

I began moving towards the figure.

As I walked, more shapes came into view. Long, lodgepole pines in uniform rows and ramrod straight. They seemed to glow green, like St. Elmo's fire. In between the trees was a white wolf, weaving among the trunks and keeping pace with me.

The figure ahead of me stopped moving and as I got closer, I saw the hulking form of Tobar. His back was towards me and when I stopped, he turned.

He smiled and his mouth was full of fangs, glistening red. He had one eye, like a cyclops, and was holding his tomahawk. It was stained with blood. Tobar smiled at me, the smile that was full of fangs and no heart.

I looked down at his feet and could see Melanie on her hands and knees.

I looked up to see the tomahawk coming down and at the same time I heard a rushing sound like a river behind me. Before Tobar could strike with the tomahawk, I felt the impact of a crashing wave of rushing water as it slammed into me and swallowed us up like the gaping jaws of a leviathan. Then nothing but darkness filled my vision as I reached out in vain for something, anything, to hold onto.

CHAPTER SEVEN

I awoke sputtering and coughing. Drenched in cold water. I looked up at Soto, the lean one, holding a bucket.

"*Buenos dias*." He said. "Time to get to work."

Melanie was gone, but the girls were still all there, some of them kept sleeping, some of them sat up quickly and then, unnoticed by Soto who had his eyes on me, lay back down, feigning sleep.

I stood up slowly and Soto stepped back, his MP5K slung across his shoulder. I considered making a grab for it, but he must have sensed the threat of being so close to me because he moved out of reach and put a hand to the stock.

He jerked his head, motioning towards the door.

The sun was barely up, and the embers from the night's fire still smoked. The air smelled of pine, but I could barely enjoy the beauty.

Tobar was nowhere in sight, which was some sort of relief. Lugo appeared to have raided the kitchen and had a handful of pastries.

I looked from Soto to Lugo. "Where's Melanie?"

Lugo shrugged, "the kitchen, where all women should be. She is making breakfast. Everyone needs their strength. We have a long hike ahead."

"A hike? Where to?" I asked.

Lugo shook his head and waggled a finger back and forth scoldingly. "That would ruin the surprise."

I looked at Soto. "You said something about work?"

Soto motioned toward the fire and the lake. "I want to cook some fish."

"So go ahead and do it." I said.

He grinned wickedly, "like your Nike slogan? Just do it?"

"Or Nephi." I said, "Just go and do it."

He didn't get it.

I leaned forward and was encouraged to see that even though they had all the guns, I had some sort of sway over them, and they instinctively stepped back.

"I'd sooner gut you like a fish than cook one for you, Soto."

Soto glowered and Lugo, trying to recover his authority, took a bite and spoke with his mouth full of muffin. "Mister Sawyer, as I am sure you have noticed we are being very, very civil. Something that you will not see from many of our compatriots. We have not harmed the girls, which is an unprecedented concession. Equally amazing, all your digits are intact. You have all your teeth, eyes, and limbs. Your fingernails are all in place, you have not been branded. You are, in a word, incredibly lucky. We can all get along. We are under strict orders to be gentle, to use the kid gloves, even with you, but you need to help us out too, otherwise acceptable losses might happen."

I ran a hand through my hair and moved to the fire. There was plenty of kindling lying around but no pieces large enough to use as a club. I got a little blaze going in no time.

"You catch that fish you wanted cooked yet?" I asked.

Soto frowned. "No."

Lugo laughed. "That's what he really needs you for, Sawyer. He can't swim, and his line is stuck."

"You're a wetback and you don't know how to swim?"

He scowled. "At least I'm not afraid of water like Tobar."

Lugo hissed at him and looked over his shoulder.

I looked from one to the other and Soto seemed to have realized his mistake and he glanced nervously around.

I didn't ask for any elaboration.

Soto showed me where he had left the fishing rod lying on the shore of the lake.

"Where did you get the rod?" I asked.

"Trailer." He said.

"Did you know him?"

"Who?" He asked.

"Stanislav."

He shrugged, "not really, he moved in some of the same circles as us, but always on the edges. He was the one who sold you out. He saw Melanie's name show up on the registration for this campground and he started sharing in the chat rooms. Your exploits last fall have made you somewhat well-known. He called us the moment you arrived. We were already mobilized. He was supposed to help capture you. We advised Stanislav not to indulge his hobby, but apparently, he did, and you chased him down."

"Is that why Tobar killed him?"

Soto nodded, and grinned. "Tobar hardly needs an excuse. He loves to kill. That one loves killing as much as he loves women, maybe more."

I looked pointedly at Soto. "No loyalty among jackals. What makes you think he won't just kill you someday, too."

Soto patted his weapon. "He works for us. He doesn't like guns, so we have superior firepower. Now quit stalling and get the hook unstuck."

I picked up the rod, giving it a little tension until the line was taut and I could see where it was snagged some thirty or forty yards offshore. I tried moving with the rod, this way and that.

Soto seemed impatient. "I already tried that, just swim out and get it."

"Why not just cut the line?" I asked.

"I couldn't find any more hooks."

I might have tried to find some other solution, but unlike Soto, I know how to swim, I like to swim, and it would serve as a bit of a bath and, hopefully, the more we delayed, the better chance the Ayres would have to get here in time with the cavalry.

"Okay." I said and started peeling off my sweater and shirt. The morning was cool, and goosebumps broke out across my arms. I tossed my clothes across a log and stepped behind a tree to strip down to my shorts. Soto moved to keep me partially in view.

"A little privacy?" I said.

Soto leered. "You shy?"

I snorted a laugh, "Put that gun down and you'll find out."

He said nothing, but I saw his grip tighten on his weapon.

I found another tree, a little further away, Soto let me go. Removing my shoes, I pulled off my jeans and all of a sudden felt a sharp, biting pain on my bare legs and feet.

I looked down and was surprised to see one of those underground nests of yellow-jackets, or wasps, or hornets or whatever. It was still early and cool, so they weren't swarming, but they were biting and stinging.

I suppressed the urge to bolt and shout, and instead straightened up, and slowly walked back, surreptitiously brushing off the offending insects with my balled-up jeans. Red welts were forming, and I didn't want Soto to notice.

Leaving the rest of my clothes and shoes on the shore, I waded in. I should have just jumped.

Always easier to go quick.

Like tearing off a Band-Aid.

It was as cold as any water I had ever been in. Icy needles probed at my skin, but it was a relief to the stings. The water was crystal clear and not very deep. Taking several quick breaths, I dove in.

The icy water was like a punch to the chest, but I swam underwater for several body lengths with dolphin kicks until I needed to come up for air.

I waved at Soto. "Pull that line tight."

He did, and I grabbed the ahold of it. Taking a breath, I followed the line down, hand over hand, about fifteen feet to the bottom. The lure was lodged in a "v" where a sunken log and a rock met. It was easy to dislodge with the right angle and would have been achievable by simply letting out more of the line and walking around to the far side of the shore.

But I had an idea to further harass and slow down our captors. I got the lure, a quality-made silver spinner, then broke the line which fortunately was not a heavy test. I swam to the surface and raised my hand triumphantly.

Soto looked pleased. I swam breaststroke back to where I could stand, and positioned myself so that Soto was between me and the wasp nest.

"The line broke, but I got the lure, you can tie it again."

Gingerly walking across the rocks in the lake, I got nearer to the shore.

With a big underhand toss, I sent the lure sailing above his head right among the trees.

"Whoops, bad throw. Better grab that before a crow, or raven, or magpie finds it. They like shiny things."

I started rubbing my chest and arms to bring warmth back. Soto looked annoyed but followed after it. I started pulling on my clothes. After a second, I heard cursing and screaming, and Soto came bursting through the trees. He had several of the little winged stingers buzzing around him. I would have expected him to dive into the water but then I remembered Lugo had said that Soto couldn't swim.

So instead, Soto just threw himself on the ground. *Stop, drop, and roll*, as if he were on fire.

At the noise, Lugo and Melanie came running. Lugo had his gun at the ready, but let it swing freely on the shoulder strap when he saw Soto.

"Bees." I said, calmly.

Lugo looked stricken. "He has allergies to bees."

Already Soto was beginning to swell and discolor. I brushed the remaining insects away and grabbed him under the arms, dragging him back towards the camp.

"Help me." I said to Lugo.

"He needs an EpiPen." Melanie said, putting a hand to her face in genuine concern. She took the protect and serve thing seriously, even when it came to bad men.

I ripped the shirt collar away from Soto's neck as the swelling began to strain at the fabric. A horrible gurgling sound was escaping his throat, and his eyes were wide with panic.

He had found the silver spinner before being stung and the barbed hooks had embedded in the palm of his hand as the pain of the insect attack and caused him to involuntarily make a fist.

"Get the first aid kit." I said to Melanie.

I propped Soto against a log near the fire. I didn't know much about anaphylaxis, but I wanted to save him, even if he was our enemy.

I guess I took the whole protect and serve thing seriously, too.

"You're going to be okay, Soto." I said.

He looked at me, his eyes pleading.

Melanie rushed off, and I could faintly hear the sounds of stirring in the cabin. I hoped none of the girls would come outside. I did not want them to see someone die.

I prayed in my heart that he would make it, but his color looked dangerously bad. Like the scene in Charlie and the Chocolate Factory with the spoiled girl.

Then Tobar drifted from the woods, as silent as smoke.

For a split-second I considered retrieving Soto's MP5K. But it was pinned underneath him as he lay on his back over the log, and I knew I couldn't retrieve it and fire before one or both of our remaining captors got to me.

Besides, I had never fired a gun like the Heckler and Koch sub-machine gun. Not that it was overly complicated, but seconds are precious, and you should never trust a weapon you haven't personally test fired.

As I undid more buttons from Soto's shirt, I surreptitiously reached into his breast pocket and retrieved the items he had confiscated from me.

Lugo was explaining to Tobar what had happened.

Melanie scrambled next to me and stuck Soto in the meat of his thigh with the EpiPen.

It wasn't long before his breathing normalized, and his swelling subsided. After he was out of the danger zone, Lugo motioned us away with his weapon.

I straightened up and stepped away from Soto as Tobar approached. Roughly hauling Soto to his feet, Tobar slapped him, sending him sprawling into the dust.

"Fool." Tobar growled, like a mean bear, hungry after hibernation.

Lugo looked incredulously at Tobar. "What did you do that for? It was an accident."

Tobar looked at me.

Lugo followed his gaze and met mine.

"What, you think I conspired with the bees? In case you forgot, Melanie and I just saved his worthless life."

Tobar drew his tomahawk, spinning it expertly, but with a lazy, casualness that was disconcerting. With his other hand, he touched the talisman around his neck.

"The spirits tell me you have done this thing. They also tell me that he will die eventually, he is weak. Do not try any more of your tricks. I can speak to beasts as well as you and they obey me better."

Melanie moved next to me, grabbing at my shoulder, and pulling me closer to her, away from what seemed like a potentially lethal showdown

Lugo, who seemed to oversee the operation, was nonetheless stymied by Tobar. Lugo and Soto must have gone way back in terms of friendship or brotherhood or whatever the ties among villains were called.

They had been wounded by Melanie in Mexico together, had probably convalesced together, and no doubt had conducted all sorts of criminal enterprises together.

Lugo looked like he might cry from relief as he helped Soto back up to his feet. They both looked warily at Tobar, like hyenas in the presence of a ravenous lion.

Tobar spun the tomahawk, tossed and caught it, before returning it to its scabbard. He looked out across the lake and spoke in a low rumble like the echoes of an earthquake.

"We go."

Lugo seemed like he was having trouble forming sentences. He gesticulated wildly at Tobar, who didn't deign to look at him.

"But how do we go now? Soto must rest and recover. We are too few for so many prisoners otherwise."

Tobar touched the talisman. "We are many. Soto will follow, or he will die."

Melanie slid her hand down the outside of my left thigh. Flattering, to be sure, but, I thought, not the time nor the place for a kiss and an embrace. Then I felt something solid fall into the tall neck of my boot.

Well, well, well, but my girl was a resourceful one.

I smiled inwardly, knowing we would get out of this before too long.

CHAPTER EIGHT

Thankfully, Soto was alive. I hadn't meant to impose a death sentence upon him. Just an attempt at haranguing and delaying them. I had been willing, even wishful of saving his life, but he was a human trafficker, a kidnapper, an attempted murderer and who knew what else. So I wouldn't have shed any tears for him, but I was glad the girls hadn't had to witness something like that.

And Melanie hadn't hesitated. She was the one who had retrieved the first-aid kit and administered the medicine.

She was a lifesaver. A first responder. A hero.

And for better or worse the chance at cutting our opposition down by a third was gone and we were still captives.

Little did I know that it was going to get much worse.

Tobar dispassionately told Soto that if he fell behind that he would be slain and cast into the water. "It is called Ghost Lake, after all." Tobar said. "You will be made to feel at home."

Then, more to himself he sighed, "we are all ghosts."

There was hardly any inflection, no cadence, it was strictly monotone. Even rumbling thunder crashed with a variety of beats. But not Tobar. His cavernous chest sounded hollow and dead.

Melanie was made to line the girls up, and, after a hasty breakfast of instant oatmeal, we were all given packs to carry with different supplies. I was given the most to haul, but it was mainly water, foodstuffs, rope, and thin, tin cooking implements. Nothing that was overtly able to be weaponized, but as they say, necessity is the mother of invention, and I had always considered myself a moderately creative person. I am pretty much a *whatever works* kind of guy.

I thought about the rope. I could use it to either strangle them or knot it into a monkey's fist.

Tobar stood some distance off looking at the lake, Soto still seemed a little green around the gills and was leaning against a tree. Lugo began binding all our wrists together in daisy chain.

"You don't want to do that." I said.

He looked angrily at me. "You'd prefer that, wouldn't you, smart guy? Easier to try and escape, huh?"

I shrugged, "your problem, not mine, *vato.*"

He stopped, the first loop still around Melanie's wrists and looked pointedly at me.

"Why don't I want to tie them up?" He asked with equal parts suspicion and exasperation.

"By all means tie us up, but not around the wrists. I take it you are not much of a outdoorsman. That's okay - not many people are.

No offense, but this isn't Tijuana, this isn't Mexico City, this isn't your typical urban environment. Not your regular smash and grab kidnapping with cars and bags over the head. I take it that this is your first slow-motion extraction. We are going to be hiking all day and possibly into the night. People need their arms to walk. It is all about balance. What if we trip on a root or a rock and we can't catch ourselves? Then you have an injured captive, and your trip is going to take even longer. My recommendation would be around the waist."

Lugo paused, looking like he was trying to come up with a retort, or deciding whether I was trying to pull one over on him. Then he shook his head from side to side and gave a resigned kind of shrug.

But he removed the rope from Melanie's wrists and instead wrapped it around her waist. Melanie was followed by Olivia, Aubrey, Kaytee, Samantha, Emeline, Ashlin, Taylor, Caeli, and Kami.

Then me.

"You get your hands tied." Lugo hissed. "I don't care if you trip and fall. We just need you alive, you don't have to be in perfect condition."

"Okay." I said and proffered my hands. A person trying to bind you will usually expect at least some resistance and will then in turn tie you up with your hands in the worst possible way, which in my case would have been behind my back. But if you simply offer your hands up willingly, you rarely have to worry about them making any adjustments to your position. I didn't cross my wrists, either, instead I kept my palms together and as he wrapped the nylon line around in a clumsy knot, I flexed my muscles and tightened the cords in my wrists. When you relax, there is a little bit of slack that can make a world of difference.

Horses will use this concept to prevent the girth from being tightened.

He was satisfied with his work and gave a signal to Tobar, who, wordlessly, began to move off into the forest. For all his casual talk about Ghost Lake and the supposed ghosts that haunted the place, he looked as though he had just seen one himself. His swarthy complexion had a distinct pallor and despite the relative coolness of the morning, I could see beads of sweat had broken out on his brow.

What in the world could scare a man like that? Was it just the water like Soto had suggested?

Lugo had indicated the marching orders, with Melanie leading our procession, followed by Soto, and me as the caboose. Lugo walked behind me, holding his MP5K in the low ready position. I was hoping for a mountain lion, or maybe a couple of she-bears like in the Old Testament, who might be hungry for a bunch of bad apples.

Our pace was slow and awkward.

Melanie was a good leader, but none of the girls were equally yoked or exactly comparable in their own physical abilities. They either stepped on one another's heels or pulled the person behind them forward into a lurching stagger. I thought singing in cadence would help them keep step, as well as bolster morale, but Lugo told us to keep quiet.

I stole a couple glances back and even with our turtle speed, the camp was soon lost to sight, and we were in the dense, sun-dappled woods. Once, when looking back, I thought I caught a flash of white moving between sun and shadow.

The wolf?

I tried to track its movement when I caught a glimpse of it again but then my toe caught on a gnarled root, and I almost fell.

"Keep going." Lugo said, prodding me with his gun.

The path was barely more than a game trail, likely blazed by the three kidnappers on their initial insertion. I made sure to shoulder any springy branches and let them whip backwards into Lugo's face whenever I could.

He gave a little more space between us.

All the while I thought about the item in my boot. A knife, presumably. I hadn't had the chance to inspect it since Melanie made her move. Lugo and Soto would be easy to bring down, but Tobar was, for all intents and purposes, indomitable.

I figured the marching order had been decided mostly at random, but it was about the worst way it could have been. Even if I managed to cut down Lugo and arm myself with the sub-machine gun, I would have to fire an unfamiliar weapon with all the possible collateral damage in between me and my next two targets.

And that was a no go.

Periodically we passed a water bottle up and down the line, along with some jerky or trail mix. Nobody else was partial to raisins, so I got my fill. Whenever the jerky came to me, I let a few scraps fall into the brush in the hopes of bringing our white shadow, the wolf, to the rescue. If nothing else, I figured he would serve as a good distraction.

If he was still following us.

We stopped infrequently but whenever we did, Tobar would tie the end of the rope nearest to Melanie around a tree before disappearing into the woods.

Lugo was having a tough time. He was not as lean as Soto was and not as inhumanly strong as Tobar. Sweat poured off his bald scalp in long rivulets that cut through the dust on his brow. He chugged water, which wasn't good. I considered telling him to take small sips, swish it around before swallowing. But the commandment to love my enemies only stretched so far. If he cramped up, then that was his problem.

The girls all seemed to be managing. There were no murmurs or complaints. I knew some of them were soccer players and some were ballet dancers. They were young and strong.

And brave.

They weren't hysterical but neither were they resigned to a grim fate. They seemed to radiate hope, not passive despair. They no doubt had the full expectation that rescue would come. One way or another.

My way if I had anything to say about it.

At one of our breaks, I sat down, holding my bound hands out in front for balance.

"So, Lugo, what's the plan?" I asked.

His head swiveled, his mouth slack. "What?"

"Where are you taking us?"

"Not far." He panted. "One or two more days and we will be at the rendezvous point and there will be no more mountaineering."

I glanced around. "I hate to break it to you, but it is going to get harder before it gets easier. We are going uphill and if you disembarked at the same place that you're planning to take us, then you boys traveled mostly downhill. We're carrying a lot of extra gear. We are going to have to lighten the load."

His eyes got mean. "We might just kill you and save ourselves the trouble later."

I grinned at him. "You certainly could try, but what makes you think Tobar won't just do that to you next? He killed Stanislav for screwing up. He has no compunctions about killing your friend if he falls behind, but so far you seem like the only one that is struggling to keep up. He doesn't seem like one of your regular crew."

He seemed to soften, whether at the recent and painful memory of his partner's ignominious near-death experience, or at the thought of him meeting a similar end. Or maybe he was only tired from hiking.

"You are right, Sawyer." He said. "He is not one of us."

"Then why is he here?" I asked.

"As you can imagine, after our failure to handle you and the lady cop in Mexico, we were relegated to the lowest rung of the ladder. This is our chance—*my* chance—to recoup the loss. But our superiors doubted our efficacy and brought in an outsider."

"You know, Melanie and I could have just as easily wasted you two that day." I said, a little quieter so the girls wouldn't overhear.

"Yes, and that was your biggest mistake, Sawyer. One you will live to regret, though, I dare say, not for too much longer." He spat.

"Yeah, you're right. I am beginning to think wounded enemies are a lot more troublesome than dead ones. But your boss can't be hellbent on revenge for your sake, I am sure he wasn't losing sleep about your injuries. So why all the fuss for us?"

He licked his lips, removing the tiny diamonds of sweat that beaded on his upper lip. "You are a wanted man, Sawyer. You seem to have become a thorn in the side of some very unpleasant people, worse than us."

"The Haitians?" I asked, remembering the men I had fought to save four teenaged girls last fall.

He grinned, crookedly. "Yes, and others, to whom the Haitians had made promises."

"And Melanie?"

His grin widened and the tip of his pink tongue stuck out between his upper and lower teeth, reminding me of how snapping turtles lure fish into their maws.

"That is personal."

"No." Tobar had appeared beside us without a sound.

He did not look out of breath or even as though he had broken a sweat. The trail dust didn't seem to stick to him either.

"I have decided. She is mine."

Lugo looked pained. "That wasn't part of the deal."

Tobar fiddled with his talisman. "I have spoken." With the lithe, fluid movement of a jaguar, he turned on his heel and resumed his position at the head of the column.

Untying the rope from around the base of a tree, he tugged, and his massive biceps strained and swelled. All of us felt the pull and had to gain our feet quickly, or risk being dragged.

How could he pull over one thousand pounds, even just a few inches?

I knew the strongmen competitions featured men pulling airliners and tractor-trailers, but Tobar didn't seem to bat an eye, showing no signs of exertion.

Once we were all up and moving, he turned and led the way.

Our path soon went from a slow and steady incline to a sharp upward turn. The trees thinned and the earth gave way to shale and scree. That is when the going got tough. For every three steps forward, we seemed to slide one step back, especially tied together as we were, there was no way to gain a sure footing with the line going either too tight or too slack both front and back of us.

Lugo was holding onto the rope tail like a lifeline, and I felt a bit like a sled dog pulling him. It seemed as though he had simply gone limp and was not putting forth the slightest bit of effort except to hold on.

I thought about trying to rip the rope from his grasp or kick him in the face to send him rolling back down the steep grade, but I just wanted to get us all back onto level ground. Tobar looked back from time to time, his face impassive, though thankfully not impatient. He could have easily dragged us up the hill, shredding us against the sharp rocks. But he just watched. His eyes staying on Melanie for far too long.

Soto seemed to have recovered sufficiently and made his way up and down the line in intervals, making sure no one was talking.

Finally, we reached the top of a ridge with a knife edge that snaked up and down through more trees. I could see several mountain meadows, as well as two smaller lakes, almost ponds. The water was a vivid and clear blue. Pristine.

A trout nosed to the surface of the nearest of the pools, sending out concentric ripples across the glassine surface.

Fish. Blissfully unaware of the landlubbers' plight.

Far away at the bottom of our climb, I thought I saw the wolf flit from light to shadow beneath the trees.

He was still with us. As a guardian, I hoped, or at least a cautious ally, and not as an opportunistic scavenger, waiting for the first of us to drop from the forced march.

Over my shoulder I spoke in hushed tones to Lugo.

"I would recommend taking him out before he finishes you and Soto off. I mean, how do you know your bosses didn't tell Tobar to just kill you two as a punishment for your defeat last fall?"

"Nice try." He huffed as he lost his breath with the effort of speaking.

"He is a bigger threat to you than I am. I will be inclined to let you go—*again*—and he would just as soon chop you into kindling."

"What do you mean, you 'will be'?"

"That's right, I am going to break out of these bands and kick the crap out of you and Soto and Tobar all up and down this mountain."

He grunted a laugh.

"Even if I wanted to be rid of him, he can't be killed, not by me and certainly not by you."

"Why is that?" I asked.

"Because." He said, his voice lowering, "He is Wendigo."

CHAPTER NINE

"Wendigo?" I asked.

Lugo nodded emphatically.

"What does that make you? A Chupacabra?"

"Laugh if you wish, Sawyer, but I am telling you the truth."

I looked at Tobar. He was still striding out in front of our procession, but he had turned his head to look at me. With his body still mostly facing front and his head swiveled around as far as he could turn, he reminded me of a great horned owl.

When he saw that I saw that he was looking, he blinked and faced forward again, his shoulders moving in time with each of his yard-long strides.

With my eyes still on the back of Tobar's head, I spoke over my shoulder to Lugo.

"How did you guys get tangled up with him? I mean, how did your bosses even find the likes of him?"

He didn't answer, just asked, "You know what a Wendigo is?"

"A legend, a monster, an evil spirit."

"A cannibal." He said.

"Keep your voice down." I said in Spanish.

"Are you afraid he will hear us?"

"No, I don't want you to scare the girls—anymore than they already are. Besides, I'm sure he can hear us no matter how low we talk. Wendigo or not, his senses seem sharp."

We said nothing for a few more miles. Here and there we startled a squirrel or grouse and once we saw a deer dart away up the path ahead of us. I saw no more signs of the white wolf, but I trusted that he was still there.

I did not want to think about why Tobar wanted to keep Melanie.

So I didn't.

We spend so much time inside our own heads and yet so many people seem to have trouble controlling their own thoughts. Every second we can have a clean slate, a *tabula rasa*, if we want, because our brains can only entertain one thought at a time.

That must be part of the reason behind the multimedia obsession. *No thoughts required.*

Instead of worst-case scenarios, I focused my thoughts on how to get free and get these girls home safely. I thought about creative endings for Tobar, Soto, and Lugo.

It brought a wry inward smile to my mind that I could conjure up nothing more absurd than a bee sting killing Soto. And maybe Lugo would just keel over from exhaustion. But what was it that had scared Tobar?

The water. It had to be.

But was it the legend behind Ghost Lake?

Or just the dihydrogen oxide?

Maybe he was a worse swimmer than Soto.

Lugo seemed to have taken the near loss of his bosom friend hard, and while I would not have been terribly broken up about Soto kicking the bucket, I was glad it had softened Lugo. Nothing like brushing shoulders with the sense of your own mortality. He seemed more talkative and less guarded. Perhaps more susceptible to influence.

All good.

"Lugo, why do you do this? Hurt and kidnap people, I mean."

He shrugged. "We are what we are."

With my bound hands, I tilted my head and rubbed my chin in mock pensiveness. Narrowing my eyes as if in deep thought, "Hmmm, are we though?"

Sarcasm does not become me. President Gordon B. Hinckley denounced it vehemently and my father made me do pushups when I was a young man if he ever heard my friends and me indulging in sarcastic expressions. But it seemed apropos in this instance.

I continued with more sincerity, "because it seems to me that people change every day. Take you for example. You lost to us in Mexico. Making you, by definition, a loser. You almost lost Soto. Again, making you a loser. Looks like your theory of our nature being unchangeable is holding, but wait, now you have the chance to be a winner. Help us, and you'll go free. Don't, and it is only a matter of time before Tobar does you in."

He jabbed me in the back with the muzzle of his gun. "Shut up, Sawyer. Look around. This is you losing. You are the loser now."

We didn't talk after that.

So much for him loosening up.

As night began to fall, the temperature dropped. I could see the girls slowing down, shorter steps, not picking their feet up as much. Tobar did not miss a beat in his pace, but he seemed to sense the general fatigue. Soto kept moving up and down the line, urging us impolitely onward. I should have made a low buzzing sound like a bunch of bees to take the starch out of him.

Eventually, Tobar paused and looked around. Apparently satisfied, he stopped us in a clearing. Below we could see a river carving its way through the mountains.

I was untied and made to kindle a fire.

We boiled water and ate the freeze-dried *du jour*.

The girls spoke in whispers, hugging one another. Melanie and I caught each other's eyes, trying to convey messages of hope and reassurance.

Tobar did not eat with us, just stalked off into the woods.

Lugo fussed over his weapon and sat with his back against a tree far enough away from us so that he could keep everyone in view at once. Soto tried to sleep, rolling back and forth uncomfortably on the ground.

After I had hung up the foodstuffs and trash away from camp, watched closely all the while by Lugo, I stretched out in the dirt by the fire. I looked up at the night sky and was comforted by the expanse of stars, lightyears away, but they seemed so close in the wild without the cities and streets with the incessant humming of artificial illumination.

People say that stars are impartial and cold, that they don't care one way or the other what happens to us. And while I don't believe in wishes on meteors, I do believe in Him who hung the moon and scattered each star with precision and purpose.

Melanie had been untied and sent by Lugo to gather some firewood. Lugo seemed to forget that Melanie was, historically, the more dangerous of us to him and Soto. She stayed close though, not venturing out into the dark while Tobar lurked.

Aubrey raised a hand, like she was in class, and asked, "Excuse me, I heard you say the other man is a Wendigo—what does that mean?"

Lugo lazily pointed the muzzle of his gun at Aubrey, squinting one-eyed down the sights.

Rolling over, I moved in front of the Aubrey, spreading my arms out to act as a human shield if he started shooting.

Lugo lowered the submachine gun. "Sit down, Sawyer." He laughed and peered around me at Aubrey. "Are you afraid of me? Was that scary having a gun pointed at you?"

Aubrey nodded slowly.

"Wendigos are much scarier, girl. They are monsters who feast on human flesh, they are stronger and faster than any man, than any ten men. And they can see in the dark. They have malevolent spiritual powers. There are not so many this far south. Tobar came from Canada. He is *Indio*. You girls are lucky I am here, otherwise he would devour you all whole. You'll be begging to stay close to me and Soto by tomorrow. So you all should be thinking about how to keep me happy."

Lugo seemed to relish the opportunity to scare a literally captive audience. He told us that once upon a time in Mexico, a group of *narcos* had been in a gunfight with some *federales* and that Tobar had slain a dozen of the policemen, single-handedly, with nothing but his tomahawk.

As he fell into his role of scary storyteller, Soto tied us all together again. I offered no resistance and waited until he sat back down. I made as if I was loosening my boots to get more comfortable for sleep. Rolling over, so that my back was to Lugo and Soto, I slipped the object that Melanie had given me out from my boot.

It was a knife indeed. A steak knife, specifically. Its serrated edge made quick work of the ropes, but I left a few strands intact. I had moved closer to the fire so that Lugo's view of me would be obscured by the dancing tongues of flame. Melanie walked behind me as far as the rope would reach, pretending like she was sweeping pinecones and needles out of the way. I caught her eye. Lugo was making semaphores of sawing and swiping motions as he described Tobar's bloodlust and violent acts. Melanie bent down to me and palmed the hilt of the knife I passed to her.

Lugo was dumb, but not that dumb. He paused in his riveting narrative. "No touching, you two, no tricks." I held my hands together like the prayer hands emoji the kids send in their text messages as an apology. The motion seemed to distract him from Melanie's own movement as she slipped the knife up her sleeve. Lugo narrowed his eyes suspiciously but continued with his tales of horror.

Soto yawned, probably having heard all the stories already, and bunched a backpack under his head to serve as a pillow.

Apparently, Tobar was a pretty spooky guy, not that we hadn't surmised as much, despite our only recent acquaintanceship.

Lugo went on about how he had seen the giant torture and kill several enemies and was beginning to describe in the greatest of detail the harvesting of various organs when I stood up again.

"Okay, Lugo, that's enough of your ridiculous imaginations. Keep it up and your miniature parade will be plagued with bad dreams, unable to sleep and exhausted tomorrow."

Melanie was gathering up the girls in what could have been perceived as a huddle for warmth or comfort or prayer but what was actually the means to the speedy severing of the ropes that linked them.

"Siéntate, Sawyer." He told me again. patted the MP5K with one hand.

"Help me roll that big log over here, it will work to keep some of the heat and, for your sake, will hide the firelight. They are probably searching for us by now."

I pointed toward a part of a fallen tree that lay near where he sat. He followed my gesture with his eyes and if I had been closer, it would have been a good opportunity to attack him.

But I waited.

Hoping Tobar wouldn't come back too soon.

Lugo sighed exasperatedly, like I was the one who was putting him out and that he was making a huge sacrifice for me.

When you stand up, you should be able to do so without using your hands. Or, at the very least, you should be able to lean back, prop yourself up on one arm, get your legs under you, and then stand up straight.

Lugo did neither. Instead, he swung the gun on the strap to his side, leaned forward onto his knees and put both hands in front of him.

Bounding forward, I planted the sole of my right boot against the side of his head. Bursting the last strands of the bands that held my hands together, I swooped down and pulled the MP5K off from around him.

Soto stirred and as he tried to sit up, I booted him hard in the head and stomped on him a couple times until he was still.

The girls, now freed, were beginning to run when suddenly they froze.

All the air seemed to suck out of the clearing, even the firelight sputtered as if from a sudden strong wind.

Tobar stood just on the edge of the firelight, his countenance seemed to change with the flames, as if there were a thousand faces behind his visage.

Without thinking, I raised the gun and pulled the trigger.

CHAPTER TEN

Lugo had set the weapon to single fire. There was a toggle for safe, single, a three-shot burst and fully automatic. The gun bucked in my hand and spat a bullet. Tobar was a big target, and while I had no wish to kill anyone—even him, it was pretty much my only course of action.

There was a *ping* of metal on metal, sparks, and the sound of the bullet ricocheting away like an angry hornet.

Tobar had deflected the bullet with the head of his tomahawk.

But that was impossible.

He wasn't that fast, right?

No, it was just that, against the odds, my un-aimed shot happened to hit Tobar's hatchet.

Stretching forth his free hand, Tobar's eyes seemed to glow red in the firelight. My ears were ringing with the shot, and I was only vaguely aware of Melanie shepherding the girls into the woods.

The weapon in my hand suddenly felt hot, like a live coal burning my palm. I dropped it instinctively. Tobar smiled, all teeth and no heart. Slowly, almost ponderously, he bent down and picked the largest stick out of the fire by the unburnt end. The fire shrunk markedly with the removal of part of its fuel.

My limbs felt leaden, and I could only stare between Tobar and the totem slung about his neck.

Tobar said something in a gravelly voice that I couldn't understand and, sheathing his tomahawk, passed a hand over the burning end of the stick. There was a flare of bright blue light, like the end of a blowtorch. I shielded my eyes against the blinding, eldritch light.

Then I understood his words and they sent waves of ice through me.

"I am filled with the spirit of Tahquitz, the first Shaman. I can make the stars fall from the sky and hold their light in my hand. He motioned with his torch, and I looked up.

Impossible.

Darkness. Inky blue blackness.

Every star was gone.

Fallen into the flame in his hand.

No, not gone. I just couldn't see them because of the stark light that blinded me to all other lights.

"I can make the earth shake." He said and must have leapt into the air because I felt the vibrations of his huge frame crashing down as he jumped and stamped.

"All will obey me." He raised the torch above his head, and it made his face look like a skull. "Children, come to me."

It was like waking up from a bad dream. I felt a crawling, dreadful fear like I had never known. It was all-consuming, maddening, a tingling, rattling sensation deep in the bones that sends shivers down the spine. I thought I could go mad with fear.

But then I caught hold upon a thought, a revelation.

The devil has no power over me.

Whatever illusions and cheap parlor tricks that this charlatan conjured up, they were no match for the Priesthood of God.

I took the poisonous fear coursing through me and forced it back, concentrating it into a single small mass and crushing it into nothing.

I spoke then, and I felt like I was suddenly not alone.

"No. You have no power here."

I stepped forward and scattered the remnants of the fire with my feet.

Tobar's torch went out.

We were cast in deep shadow and the stars seemed to have been turned back on.

Springing forward, I threw a short right uppercut to his body and felt like I had hit a the side of a brick storehouse.

Trying an overhand left, I missed in the gloom and felt a huge fist graze my collarbone. It was not a clean hit, but even so I felt like I had been clubbed with a sledgehammer. I spun away and tried to make out his shadow against the trees and sky, wondering if he really could see in the dark.

Remembering that he was right-handed, I moved to my right, away from his strong side. As I took my first step, I felt the *whoosh* of an elbow as it whistled by my left shoulder in a crushing arc.

Wildly, I let go with an overhand right, like a trebuchet. Making partial contact with his chin, I felt no give, no wince, no recoil.

I might as well have hit the hull of a battleship.

I pressed, charging with a left elbow at shoulder height to me, which was midriff high to him. I sensed his intricate musculature bunch on impact with my strike, effectively dispelling my attack. I stayed close, hoping to mitigate his reach and discourage the use of the tomahawk.

But his size was surpassed only by his strength and his left hand clamped down behind my head and I was tossed head over heels with the ease of a child throwing a balled-up pair of socks into a laundry hamper.

If I stayed down, I would be dead, no matter how high value a prize I was to Lugo's employers. Rolling away as fast I could manage. I passed through the underbrush and dust. I heard his footsteps, like those of the Giant in Jack and the Beanstalk, moving in pursuit.

Thinking more and more about Lugo's assertion that Wendigos could see in the dark, I came to a crouch. Keeping my hands in front of my face, so as not to garrote myself on a low-hanging tree limb, I felt my way around the trunk of a tree.

I tried to quiet my thumping heart and incoming breath.

I heard nothing.

No stalking monster, no fleeing children, no groanings from Lugo or Soto.

It was too dark to see.

I shot a quick look up between the close-knit treetops to the distant stars, tried to pull the light from them to illuminate the woods.

Closing my eyes to sharpen my other senses, I reached out into the darkness with my ears, willing the stars to fall right on Tobar's head.

And most important of all, I prayed.

When I was a missionary in Peru, a general authority, Elder Uceda, visited our mission and asked me what I thought a "mighty prayer" entailed.

Thinking of Enos in the Book of Mormon and his prayer that lasted all day and all night, I answered that a "mighty prayer" would generally be much longer than usual.

Gently, but powerfully, he corrected me. He related a story from his own missionary days when he had a near-death experience on the trails at Machu Pichu, and his "mighty prayer" was just a single word; *Help.*

Such was my own prayer, now.

There was a hiss, and without thinking I ducked and rolled as the tomahawk *thunked* into the trunk right where I had been.

Good. Now he was without his preferred armament.

Staying low, I scanned the forest against the slightly brighter backdrop of the skyline. Spotting a shadow that looked like a tree, but wider, I charged.

His arms started to come up to get hold of me, but I juked left then right, coming up on his left and planting a right uppercut to his ribs. The punch was perfect, starting from the ground up, my feet planted, my hips twisting and my fist digging into the move. It should have broken or cracked a dozen ribs. It would have lifted lesser men off their feet and dropped them to their knees. But Tobar barely budged.

With awful dread, I realized that I couldn't hurt him.

I didn't see his left fist, like a ship's yardarm, come swinging in a backhand strike. It caught me full in the face and I fell back, bounced off a tree only to be hit in the stomach by another crushing punch from Tobar. It felt like his knuckles would go all the way through my guts and touch my vertebrae.

I sank to one knee, unable to breathe. Trying to stand, I was instead lifted, all two-hundred pounds of me, picked up off the ground by the throat. His arms were so long, I could barely reach to kick him.

When fighting someone bigger and stronger than you, it is essential to remember that it is not your whole body against their whole body. That is a fight you'll often lose. Instead, it is your whole body against their groin, their eyes, their fingers.

A single, vulnerable target at a time.

He wasn't strangling me quite yet. Just toying with me. Meanwhile, I struggled to get ahold of his fingers to jerk them from side to side and break them off like husks of corn from the stalk. Instead of panicking at the prospect of broken fingers and releasing me, he just squeezed harder.

There are two kinds of chokes, air and blood. An airway choke cuts off your oxygen supply and is frontal pressure, a blood choke cuts off the circulation to the brain and is applied to the sides of the neck. Tobar opted for the latter and as he crushed my carotid arteries, my vision ebbed into streaks of red and black.

Like staring into the campfire, I thought.

It can only take a few seconds for a good choke to work and even though I had a strong neck and had never been submitted when grappling competitively, I felt myself slipping.

Sparks.

Fluttering into the brightness of life before dimming and dying.

Here I was again, on the brink of death and there was still no lifetime flashing before my eyes. Instead, certain moments, the really important ones, and the people who matter most, sort of fade in and out, backlit, haloed, and framed. Like those old picture slide machines that click and clack at the pull of a lever making the next shot come into view, and you adjust the focus on the projector until it is just about right.

I saw my parents, my siblings and their families, I saw far-off distant faces and places, from my mission to Peru. I saw my high school English teacher, Mr. Rice, I saw Melanie and the Ayres. I saw my mission companions, my first boxing coach, neighbors and friends. Extended family, aunts, uncles, and cousins. I saw my grandparents, gone too soon. They weren't old like I remembered them, but young and fit, just like in the photographs framed on my mom's mantle.

Then Melanie was back in the foreground of my mind. I was glad she got to make a double appearance. There was so much I wanted to say. So much I wanted to do. I had to ask her something. Something important, but I couldn't remember, not right then. It would come to me if I could just hold on.

The lights went down further, like in a movie theatre before the feature film.

Let's all go to the lobby and buy ourselves some snacks.

Melanie was swinging some sort of improvised club. She probably would have made a good softball player. There were flashing lights like at a Tacoma Rainiers game. I liked watching ball games—the great American pastime—but I couldn't play it very well.

My dad on the other hand was a great ballplayer.

There was a cheer from the crowd that sounded like a dull roar as Melanie hit a homerun.

Maybe these visions weren't strictly memories but ideas, possibilities and hypotheticals. Maybe there was no rhyme or reason to them.

Suddenly it was full dark, no more peanuts and crackerjacks, but I could still make out Melanie, swinging away with what looked like a tree branch.

There had been an almost complete absence of sound when seeing each freeze frame from my life, but now it came rushing back into my ears and I felt like I could see better than ever, even though it was still dark.

Melanie was there, battering Tobar wherever she could reach him with her weapon. He didn't seem to pay much attention, but finally he turned his head, slowly, like a glacial encroachment, and with an equally precise but infinitely faster motion, he let go of me and caught the end of her stick mid-swing. I slumped to the ground in a heap and watched t as he jabbed the branch downward, causing it to slip through Melanie's hands and hit her in the stomach.

Struggling to my feet, I started to lunge but Tobar swung the stick backhanded at me. The end of it caught me under the chin. My teeth clacked together, and my head rocked back. I got another perfect view of the stars through the trees for a split second and then I was moving backwards.

And down.

I hadn't realized how close we had maneuvered to the edge of the steep hillside. One moment my feet were finding the ground and then as I took another step back there was nothing.

I felt the sinking, sickening feeling experienced on rollercoasters or going too fast up and down hills on the road in your car.

Suddenly I was airborne, but not for long. My shoulders hit first, and I slid down the shale. Rolling, I passed through shrubbery, grabbing for a handhold on any exposed root or branch. I uprooted several species of the local flora. Once I bounced off a stout tree that knocked the wind out of me like Tobar's punch. My leg got caught in some brush that slowed my tumble but not enough to arrest it.

Down, down I rolled. Tail over teakettle. Starting miniature avalanches of small rocks. I tried to get my hands up and over my head to protect myself, but with each cartwheel I instinctively reached out to try and catch myself somewhere, anywhere.

In some places the slope turned sheer, and I fell a few feet straight down, bouncing off my shoulders and elbows.

I was still too pumped up with adrenaline to feel the cuts, bumps, and abrasions, but they were there. And multiplying. Each one patiently waiting to send their waves of pain scorching through my nerve endings.

I got no more visitations from the people who made my life so enchanted, which might have been a good sign that I wasn't going to die yet.

I heard a new rushing sound, not the blood pounding in my ears, but something louder, and further away but closing fast.

The river.

At the exact time I realized where I was headed, I hit the water.

Ice cold. It came crashing over me, tumbled me like a bunch of clothes in a washing machine. I scraped across the bottom, my fingers slipping on smooth, slippery stones. The water turned shallow and I broke the surface, gulping air as the current turned me around so my feet were pointed downstream. I dug my heels in, skidding and sliding, like a cartoon roadrunner.

Fumbling for the bank, I slipped, splashed underwater, **an**d rose again to the sandy riverbank.

The stars were bright, and I was out of the woods along a clear stretch where river rocks in all shapes and sizes covered the ground for fifty yards on either side of the water before the tree line.

I was shivering and cold and while the water did much to numb the wounds from the fight and the fall, I could barely move.

I stumbled forward, caught myself against the trunk of a massive fallen tree, grayed by age and washed downstream long ago.

I was very tired. I felt myself falling again, like you do in dreams, only this time the sensation did not wake me up like it often does in dreams.

This freefall put me fast asleep.

Moyobamba, San Martin, Peru: 2 years before

The prison was far out of town. We walked for almost an hour down a single-track dirt road, rutted and rough, that threaded through groves of scrub trees and across wide fields of tall grass. At length we caught a glimpse of the prison. Though newly constructed, the four-storied building appeared as spartan as any ancient dungeon beneath the castle of some minor lord. No gleaming light poles or fresh-painted gates. Just blank concrete and raw metal doors already starting to spot with rust. The whole thing emanated an unsettling and forbidding feeling.

Maybe that was the whole point.

Even though the guards seemed competent, they gave us only a cursory glance, perhaps reassured by our white shirts, ties, and name badges. Religious ministrations still carried some weight in a predominantly Christian country.

We made our inquiries at the reception desk and were informed that Anibal was on the first floor. The desk guard called for his partner who was on patrol on one of the higher floors but returned shortly to lead our way.

We were shown down a long bare hallway lit with single bulbs in wire cages every twenty feet or so. The inside was even less appealing than the outside. The heavy metal doors that lined the hall were already rusted and stained. Perhaps recycled from an older, now defunct facility. Water ran underneath a couple of doors and pooled in the hallway.

From the various cells came voices. The yells, sobs, and moans that together form a discordant symphony of complaint, menace, and misery.

And the smell was terrible.

The patrol guard rapped on the door at the end of the hall and unlocked a thin slot low down on the door that would have served to pass meal trays through.

I noticed that he wore an incongruously elaborate watch on his right hand. Genuine gold with several dials.

Many missionaries had been robbed for their watches.

There were plenty of bootlegging outfits in Peru that would make knock-off designer clothes and jewelry. I wasn't an expert, but it looked like the real article.

An Omega Speedmaster. Had to be worth more than he made in a year.

Maybe he had confiscated it from some rich criminal that had incarcerated.

The guard walked away, exchanging harsh words with some of the inmates and peering through the scratched viewing windows at others.

The slat opened and a pair of dark, watery eyes flitted between us and seemed to brighten.

"Elders." He said.

"Brother Anibal, we wanted to come visit you."

"The Bishop sent us." Geronimo added.

A semblance of a smile crossed his face as Anibal quoted Matthew chapter twenty-five, verse thirty-six. "I was in prison, and ye came unto me."

I had been taken away in the back of a police car from high school one time. A simple misunderstanding and even though I had not gone to juvenile detention, I had spent an inordinate amount of time in a windowless interrogation room.

At least there had been carpet and air conditioning.

I could not imagine how it would feel to be on the other side of that door.

"Brother Anibal, what can we do for you?"

"A prayer, perhaps?" Geronimo suggested.

He nodded and fished his fingers out through the narrow opening. Geronimo and I each grasped a hand of his and I offered a prayer.

I hoped that it had not sounded half-hearted, but I didn't know what to say. I thought ruefully of Joseph who was sold into Egypt, Paul and Silas in the book of Acts, Alma and Amulek in the Book of Mormon, and Joseph Smith in Liberty Jail. Could Anibal expect any of the same miracles?

I realized that we did not know what he was even in for.

But that seemed like an insensitive question.

He must have read my mind because his eyes bore into mine and he whispered, "I didn't kill those people."

CHAPTER ELEVEN

I awoke just before dawn and for a long blank moment I couldn't grasp any of the who, what, and where of me. I was frightened a little, with no sense of time, place, or identity.

Then it all came back in a rush, and I was frightened a lot.

Not for myself, but for the girls.

I could feel the aches and pains distinctly. Moving cautiously, I assessed the damage and found a lengthy list of injuries but all of them minor. I breathed a sigh of relief and a prayer of gratitude that I had suffered nothing that would put me out of commission. I patted my pockets to make sure I still had my things that I had reclaimed from Soto.

I did.

Miraculously.

I removed my pocket-sized Book of Mormon, passport, and a wad of cash. All soggy. I hoped the sun would dry them out.

Unable to stand, I tried to sit and instead slipped partway back into the water and all the way back into a restless sleep, I dreamed of falling. Falling from out of planes and over cliffs, as well as through windows, off rooftops, and down sheer rock faces. I dreamed of being swept down a dark and muddy river with great, big crocodiles lining the banks.

I dreamed that the moon had a face. But not that of a man. This was more animalistic. Large, luminous eyes that shined in the dark and a long snout. The moon began to set but not towards the horizon. It came straight down towards me, huge and white, the mouth opened and there were rows of giant fangs as big and white as snowcapped mountain peaks.

I felt pain in my shoulder as the jaws clamped down—I didn't know I could feel anything in a dream. There was supposed to be less gravity on the moon, but some cold, rushing, inextricable force seemed to pull at my legs, while the moon tore at my upper half.

Then I was dragged over moonstones, and I felt them bounce along my back. Then the moon let go, and whatever had been tugging at my legs released me as well.

I opened my eyes at the first lick. Closed them at once. The wolf had found me and was lapping me up like a Tootsie Roll Pop. *How many licks to get to the center?*

He had pulled me from the water. But to what end? To devour me like a soggy sandwich?

I brought my hands up to fend off the assault and felt the wounds and bruises all over again. The sun was high, but the wolf stood in such a way that I was in his shadow. The massive furry head retracted, tilting to the side in curiosity. I blinked as the sunlight found my face.

He was larger than I had thought, as tall and big-boned as a mastiff but woefully thin, almost greyhound-like. His fur was white and long, dark at the ends from dirt, giving that dye effect some girls like to get done to their hair—ombré, I think it's called.

His ears didn't seem quite right. They were on top of his head, more like a German Shepherd than strictly lupine.

That is when I noticed the collar.

It was wide and tight and old.

I couldn't even get a finger underneath it. When I touched the collar, he flinched and growled low, lifting a lip, exposing a set of jagged teeth.

"Easy, boy." I said standing up shakily. "I have to get this off you, or you're going to starve or suffocate." Still unconvinced, he tossed his head like a horse avoiding a bridle, but he didn't move away.

The collar was made of plain leather, cracked with sun, rain, and age. The buckle was rusty, but I managed to undue the clasp it and slip it off.

He jumped and swapped ends, snuffling with delight. Playfully, he put his forepaws out in front, bending down and keeping his hindquarters up. Jumping from side to side, he suddenly rushed in. Nuzzling against me, weaving in between my legs.

A bony hip bumped against my right knee, sending a shot of pain crackling like chain lightning up my leg. I winced, and nearly fell.

Oh yeah. I remembered. *I have sustained some injuries.*

"Settle down, boy." I said, lowering myself onto the ground, my back against a log.

The collar was still in my hand, and I inspected it. It had been cinched nearly to the tightest spot. There was no nametag with a phone number or proof of rabies shots dangling from the metal ring, but I figured there might have been one that had come off some time ago. He must have been lost or abandoned when he was a puppy.

"What's your name, boy?"

I tried to think up a good moniker for my new friend. I imagined him responding in a dog voice, like Scooby-Doo, or something. But that did not seem to suit him. Maybe more like a grizzled old cowboy. Like Sam Elliot.

Shadow, grrrrufff.

"Shadow? Shadow, that's a good name."

His tongue lolled out his mouth and he sat panting for a minute, before getting up to sniff something out.

Of course it's a good name. It's mine.

Doing a mental inventory, I again ran a head-to-toe exam on myself, checking and confirming the extent of my wounds.

I had several cuts and scrapes that would need cleaning. Eventually. Injuries that occur in the wild, and especially at altitude, do not fester as quickly as those sustained in crowded cities.

Bruises galore riddled almost every inch of easily accessible soft tissue. I wasn't too worried about those. The only thing that had me bothered was my knee.

And not because I was heartbroken at the prospect of not being able to become a professional soccer player or having to go through weeks of physical therapy. No, it was that I still had to get back up the mountain and rescue the girls and then hike out of here.

Pain was one thing. Pain is almost always manageable. But mechanics are mechanics and if something just won't work, you can't make it do anything, pain or no pain.

Flexing my knee gently, extending and bending it, I didn't get the sense of any popping, clicking, or grinding. There seemed to be a bit of swelling and the outside of my knee was tender to the touch. That was where Shadow had rubbed against.

Gingerly, I walked around tested my weight and took a few running steps.

All good.

I figured as long as I didn't bump it or fall off a cliff again, I should be good to go. My clothes were still wet, and my boots squelched with each tentative step.

Even though the sun was warm, I knew that hypothermia was a legitimate concern, but I really didn't have time to sit around cooling my heels or rather *warming* them. The thing to do after cold exposure is to get the blood flowing. Pushups, pull ups, a hard run. But I didn't think my knee would stand up to that kind of activity. I wanted to keep any bursts of speed in reserve for when the real action started.

Whenever that might be.

Unfortunately, I had ended up on the wrong side of the river. I could see in the distance the ridge where I had fallen from. At least, I thought it was the right one. I had no idea what time it was or what was going on up there.

Whether Melanie and the girls had escaped.

Or if they were much worse off.

What had I said to Melanie just two nights ago? *The what ifs will tear us to bits.*

I shook my head and it hurt a little. I could feel water sloshing around in my ear. I hopped on my one good leg to get it out.

Shadow trotted along beside me, zigzagging around.

"We have to get you something to eat, boy. You're wasting away."

I could certainly eat, I wouldn't mind a bit of bacon or a nice, rare steak.

I felt in my pockets for any scraps or crumbs and found a few sodden peanuts from a pack of trail mix. None of those colorful chocolate circles. Sugar weakens the legs, and I didn't have a lot of strength to spare at the moment.

It was going to be an arduous climb back up to where we had been, but this time I was not hampered by restraints or a heavy backpack.

Then a thought occurred to me. We had been following the river for most of our forced march. I was some ways ahead of them since the trail had just as many, if not more, twists and turns as the river.

They just might come to me.

But where would the trail come closest to the river? And when should I cross the river and where?

"You found us before, Shadow, can you find the group again?"

Oh, man of little faith, of course I can, but first I must sniff these tree trunks.

We continued on, making pretty good time, or so I thought. But it was all relative. It depended entirely on the girls' situation. Where were they? Where was Tobar?

Real violence exists. And not only exists, but it also thrives in some circles. Sometimes just below the surface like a nest of snakes, writhing, coiling, and hissing. Dry scales rubbing over dry scales.

In some places violence stands out and walks around, loud and proud, big as life and twice as ugly. It isn't limited to back alleys of busy urban areas. Nor is it confined to war zones in distant lands. It can rear its head anywhere and at any time.

If we're lucky it never finds us. It doesn't find most of us. Most people go through life without so much as a fistfight, let alone lethal encounters. But real, unadulterated violence was here now. And while I was no stranger to it, I knew that I was at a disadvantage because I did not want to kill my enemies and they had no such inhibitions.

I had always relied on my sure knowledge that God would protect us. And He always had. But it has ever been the case that terrible things can happen to good people. Faith in God does not mean that you suddenly turn ten feet tall and bulletproof.

I wasn't sure that I could beat these guys in my present condition unless I came at them with something more than plucky courage and a winning smile.

"How did you end up here, anyway, Shadow?"

How did you end up here?

"That is a good a question, buddy, a real good question."

He gave me a funny look. He didn't raise an eyebrow, but he reminded me a little of Melanie, not as cute, but just as critical of my conversational skills, or lack thereof.

I wondered how much of what I said he could understand. Not much. But I figured that he got the gist of it.

We found a series of small game trails that paralleled the riverbank. I didn't want to be seen from the mountain, so we stayed well back beneath the tree cover, but still within sight of the water. Shadow looked like he was on to something, maybe he had discovered a nice and tidy escape route for all of us, but it was probably just a rabbit.

I followed with less ease, pushing through brambles and low tree limbs. I slid once in a streak of mud and moss. My knee twinged and I had to haul myself up using a stout stick. I kept it to use as a dual-purposed walking-stick/weapon.

"Do you mind slowing down a bit, Shadow?"

He glanced back, then continued his long loping way.

Ah, frail youth, truly the spirit is willing, but the flesh is weak. I am going as slowly as I possibly can without gathering moss. Is that the human expression? Or is it, a rolling stone catches the worm, *and,* the early bird gathers no moss? *I am not partial to stones or worms or birds myself. Unless it is a nice grouse.*

"Tell you what, old boy, if you get us out of this, I'll buy you the biggest ham you've ever seen."

He did not acknowledge my offer, just kept darting away, finally pausing when he was nearly of sight.

We kept on like that for the better part of an hour when he suddenly darted out of the trees onto the rock-strewn bank of the river.

"Shadow, wait!" I called, not wanting him to be spotted.

He paid me no mind and just ran to the water's edge, pointing like a birddog to the far side of the river.

I saw it, too.

The clear sign of a trail.

I had no doubt the mountains were crisscrossed and checkerboarded with all sorts of fire access, logging roads, game, and hiking paths, but Shadow seemed so confident. This appeared to be a spot where the ridges and spurs of the mountains let out into deep draws that funneled our way.

"Are they coming here? Or have they already passed through?"

Shadow looked at me like I was an idiot.

If they had already gone through, why would I bring you here?

"Good point."

I knew Shadow could swim since he had pulled me from the river, but I wasn't sure if we should cross for reconnaissance or wait here to stage an ambush.

"The question is," I said out loud, "whether or not they are all together or split into groups."

I figured if the girls had escaped, they would have gone back the way we had come, not further into unknown and potentially hostile territory. But if they had been recaptured, the bad guys were sure to bring everybody this way.

Shadow panted, then stood up and lapped some water from the stream.

I moved along the bank, inspecting the edges. Directly across from the draw, the river widened but also ran shallower. The large river rocks gave way to smaller stones and gravel. Plenty of driftwood had piled up here and there. It seemed like an ideal crossing place before the river rushed into rapids just a little way downstream.

Upstream, the way Shadow and I had come, there was a dam of sorts, made from all the flotsam and jetsam of the river, growing and shrinking throughout the seasons. It didn't stop the flow by any means, but it lessened the level enough, like kinking a fire hose.

A plan began to develop in my mind. The river might be the gate to separate the girls from the boys. I knew Tobar was afraid of at least the lake water, and Soto couldn't swim. I knew Lugo to be out of shape, but I didn't know how he would fare in the water.

Perhaps Tobar's bloodlust and determination might overcome his fear enough to allow him to ford the river at a shallow spot, but if I could somehow forestall Tobar, get the girls across, and then unstop the dam...

I scouted back upstream. Part of a long-dead tree had buried the remains of its root mass on the far side of the bank and made up a good part of the miniature dam. With a long step, I got on top of it, testing its integrity. I walked to the opposite bank, then back again.

I was heavier than any of the girls, so I figured we were good to go.

Except Tobar had been leading the procession previously, and if that were still the case, Shadow and I would have to create some sort of distraction.

Absently, I twirled my walking stick, trying to figure out our plan of attack.

My hairbrained scheming session was cut short when I saw Shadow's ears twitch, and heard a low growl rumble out of him like a distant avalanche.

CHAPTER TWELVE

Clicking my tongue at Shadow, he and I retreated behind the tree line and waited. Pretty soon we caught a glimpse of movement and the flash of inorganic colors. Lugo and Soto, each looking a little worse for wear after being treated to my kicks, came down the trail at the sort of low-speed run that is more of a stumble when you are not used to the momentum of going downhill.

They had their guns slung across their chests and they windmilled their arms for balance. Behind them came Melanie, Kami, Kaytee, Olivia, Aubrey, Ashlin, Samantha, Taylor, Caeli and Emeline.

Shoot. They got recaptured.

None of them were tied up, though. Which was good. It would make our second great escape that much easier. I guess our captors forgot to pack extra rope.

Once Lugo and Soto reached the bottom of the trail they turned to watch as the girls took a more cautious descent down the steep decline. The pair of *bandidos* were holding their guns at the ready and looking out across the scene.

I waited for Tobar to come into view.

He didn't.

Not good.

I couldn't imagine a scenario where Melanie had managed to clobber Tobar, or that he had sprained an ankle or died of dysentery. He had to be out there somewhere. Scouting ahead maybe or wrestling a bear.

I fought the urge to look behind me. Like when you are home alone or walking at night and you *know* that there is no one there, but you just have to make sure.

My neck hairs prickled, but Shadow would have reacted if we were being stalked. For all of Tobar's powers I didn't think that he could surpass Shadow's senses. It was nice having the dog around.

I gave in and looked around.

All clear.

Lugo sat down heavily on a big rock, arching his back and yanking off his boots to massage his feet.

The girls looked tired, and I could see, even from a hundred yards away, that Melanie had a welt under one eye.

I grit my teeth together, tightening my grip on my walking stick.

They had hit my girl.

Soto checked his watch, looked around.

Kami was distributing some snacks and sips of water. No one spoke.

"Shadow, I have an idea." I whispered.

Well, imagine that. A human with an idea. Just make it snappy or I'll have to take charge of this situation.

I held up a hand in the *stay* motion. Shadow looked at me like I was an idiot but sat dutifully still. I crept back through the woods until I was sure that I would be out of sight of the group. Then I slunk back into the water. The dam was going to be a problem because the tendency is to get sucked under and held by the current, especially if I was playing possum. I would have to play it smart and time it right.

I took several deep breaths, then several rapid ones. Then I lay face down and let the current take me.

I tried to look like I was either dead or unconscious but when I reached the dam, I needed another breath, so I inconspicuously slid an arm over the top and levered myself over and inhaled. I slapped onto the water again and tried to steer myself to the edge. The water level dropped, and I scraped bottom, propelling myself forward with my toes until I was just barely out of the water and tried to breathe without moving.

I was face down and I heard one of the girls cry out and Melanie's sharp intake of breath.

Lugo shouted, "everyone shut up. Sit down and do not move. Soto, let's check it out. Maybe he's still alive, eh?"

Perfect.

My plan would only work so long as they both came together.

I heard the click of their hurried steps across the rocks. I tried to visualize their relative positions in my mind. Someone, Soto, maybe, squatted next to me and I felt rough hands roll me over. I tried to seem limp, pliable, and dead.

"He's dead." Lugo said.

I smirked inwardly.

There was a shifting sound, their guns being swung around to their backs.

"Check for a heartbeat, or something?" Soto asked.

My eyes were closed and through my lids I felt the heat and light of the sun burning orange through the darkness. Then that light was blotted out by their shadows as they leaned over me.

I had to move before they tried to give me mouth to mouth resuscitation.

Like a rattrap suddenly sprung, I shot out both hands and grabbed them by the front of their shirts. They didn't even have time to scream at the reanimated corpse grabbing at their throats before I jerked them forward, clunking their heads together with a meaty, echoey sound, like two stones knocking against each other under water.

They both slumped over. Out cold.

But for how long?

Scrambling up to my feet, I grinned at the girls.

Melanie had a hand over her mouth and tears in her eyes. She ran to me and kissed me fiercely on the lips. I hugged her and motioned the girls to me.

"Tobar was right behind us." Melanie said breathlessly, looking back up the trail.

"We don't have much time. We're going to get across the river." I pointed towards the dam where we would make the crossing. Melanie nodded and started to move for the MP5s.

Then Shadow started barking furiously.

Someone screamed.

I turned and saw Tobar coming out of the trees, like the old footage of Sasquatch. He saw us and didn't change speed. Just kept on coming, like a juggernaut.

"Go, go! Melanie, forget about the guns."

We made straight for the dam, stumbling across loose rocks. Kami and Kaytee made it to the log bridge first and hurried across. Aubrey helped Olivia and Emeline get ahead of her and Samantha held Ashlin's hand.

They bunched up on the other side, as Shadow moved toward them, still barking.

"It's okay," I called to them, "he's friendly."

Tobar wasn't, though. He had unsheathed his tomahawk but had slowed his approach and was eyeing the water warily.

That's right you big ugly monster, you can't get across the water.

Soto and Lugo were coming around to consciousness.

I saw them pulling their guns around and gingerly touching their foreheads, checking for blood.

Tobar was calling to them.

"Kill him, you fools. Kill him now."

I didn't look to see if they raised their guns or not. I just kept moving.

I pulled Melanie onto the log behind me. The log shifted and settled. The girls' traffic had loosened the root mass, and the trunk now had water running over the top of it in places.

We were a little more than halfway across when the log shuddered, and I feared it might break loose entirely. I turned around and saw Soto, trying to get a footing. He let go of his gun and held out his arms like a tight-rope walker. Lugo was coming up behind him, peering around his partner as if looking for a clear shot.

Tobar, his eyes bulging with anger or fear or both, was pacing the bank like a tiger behind the glass at the zoo. The cords on his neck stood out like the rigging on a pirate ship. In one fist he gripped his talisman. In the other he held his tomahawk, ready to throw.

I wanted to place myself between Melanie and the bad guys, but the log wasn't wide enough, or sturdy enough, for us to swap positions.

Suddenly, Melanie shoved me, hard. I fell, cartwheeling my arms. I landed sprawled out on the bank. Then, to my horror, Melanie jumped up, landing with a crash, and slipping on the log as it dislodged. She and the two pursuers spilled into the river as the loosened log set off a chain reaction and the partially choked river opened up with a rush.

The ensuing wave splashed high enough up on the back to hit Tobar and he let loose an inhuman shriek. I couldn't see Melanie. The girls had spread out on our side of the bank but stepped back as the water level rose. Shadow dashed back and forth, still barking.

I motioned to the girls with the edge of my hand in a chopping motion,

"Go, go!"

Wading into the water, I splashed around looking for Melanie to break the surface and was nearly swept off my feet by the suddenly surging current.

Tobar sprang back further from the water as the spot where he had been standing was quickly submerged. Lugo broke the surface like a breeching porpoise, and then Soto appeared, staggering, with one arm searching for balance and the other holding Melanie by the collar as he pulled her onto the opposite bank with him. Tobar reached for her with his massive paw.

I moved towards them and slipped on an algae-covered stone. I went under, popping up several yards further downstream. I came up gasping. Tobar was already pulling Melanie into the trees, and Lugo and Soto peppered the ground and the river with shots. I ducked under water again and could see bullets hit with trails of bubbles, like miniature torpedoes.

Swimming with the current I got out of range around a bend in the river.

Debris floated all around me and it was only a matter of time before I would be swept even further away. I half-swam, half-stepped back to dry land. I had moved far downstream, but the girls had tracked my movement from the trees and now they moved to help me out onto the shore.

I stood up, breathing heavily.

No time to rest. Time to go to work.

What had Melanie said to me? *Don't recriminate, just fix it.*

"Kami, can you and Kaytee get an inventory of any and all supplies, let's turn out all our pockets."

I turned to Aubrey and Olivia. "Did you see which way they took Melanie?"

They both shook their heads, shaken, crestfallen, but functioning.

"We just got into the trees and went after you. We thought you'd been shot." Aubrey said.

Shadow started nuzzling them, and they scratched behind his ears absently.

I moved back around the bend into the river to look back where we had come from.

No sign of them.

Well, shoot.

CHAPTER THIRTEEN

We didn't have much. A couple bits of food and a heart-shaped rock that Olivia collected. She said her mom liked them.

We had moved away from the water into the trees, not only to get out of the way of any more potshots from Soto and Lugo if they followed us downstream, but also so that we could hear ourselves think. The river was loud.

I ran my hands through my hair and scratched pensively at my unshaved chin.

"Brother Sawyer?" Ashlin said, "I think you're bleeding."

She pointed toward the side of my head, and I touched a spot on the top of my left ear. My fingers came away bloody. Funny, I didn't feel anything. One of the bullets must have gotten pretty darn close. I wiped my hand on my pants and shrugged. Just a scratch.

"Okay, girls, listen up" I said.

They had sat down and looked exhausted but to their credit they were attentive and tough.

"We have one task to do, and that is to get you all home safely. Melanie is smart and resourceful. She is the strongest woman I know and as soon as you all are safe, I am going to go get her."

Some of the girls exchanged looks and finally Kaytee asked, "which way do we go?"

"Back the way we came. But on this side of the river. As far as we can. Shadow will guide us, and the Ayres will be there with help by now." At my mention of his newly minted name, Shadow came up to me and licked my hand.

"We will have to walk until the sun starts getting low and then we will make a fire. Try and find any branches you can use as walking sticks, or anything else that might be useful, but don't dawdle. And no rushing willy-nilly. We don't need any slips or sprains, just purposeful movement."

The best thing in almost every situation is action, moving forward, building momentum. It is only when we stew that we despair.

We moved off in a loose file, stepping carefully, watching out for each other, holding back branches from whipping into the people behind us.

As usual, Shadow ran zigzagging ahead, finding the best routes.

Kami walked alongside me, gripping her length of wood like an infantryman holds his rifle at the low-ready, or as though it were a spear, and she were readying herself to skewer a mammoth or sabretooth tiger. She kept scanning the woods around us.

"Relax, Kami. We're in the clear for now."

She glanced at me, straightened up and twirled the stick expertly, like a baton.

"Why did Sister Clark do that? She could be here with us now."

I was asking myself the same thing. Actually, I was asking myself how I could have been so stupid, so slow, as to allow her the chance to sacrifice herself.

It should have been me.

"She is brave, and she knew what she was doing. She and I would die for you all. She is going to be okay. If they had wanted to hurt any of you, they would have done it already."

"I guess so."

"What happened? After I fell off the cliff last night? How did you get captured again?"

"Well, we thought you were dead. Sister Clark was being held by Tobar and the other two said they would shoot her if we didn't come out, so we all did. It's better to trapped together than free but alone."

I considered that.

Kami continued, "we prayed for you, though. We thought you didn't make it, but Sister Clark said that you would be okay and that you were too stubborn and too dumb to die. That made those men really angry, especially that big one, Tobar. The other two kind of got between him and us and talked him down. We prayed for them, too. I think they liked that. They didn't say anything, but they sort of smiled at us and didn't bother us when we huddled up and sang some hymns."

"Woah, sounds like you really were winning hearts and minds."

"What's that mean?"

"Never mind. Too bad they didn't just surrender to you."

We didn't say anything for a little while and then Aubrey caught up with us.

"I think some of the girls are getting pretty tired and it looks like it is going to be dark soon."

Holding up my hands, I addressed the group. "Okay everyone, this looks like as good a spot as any. Try to rest and I'll get a fire going.

But they didn't just flop down in the dirt, even though I could see they were on the verge of collapse. Instead, they started clearing an area, making it free of brush and bramble. They gathered more kindling and firewood and even found some wild radishes to supplement our meager rations.

Shadow sniffed and darted around playfully. He was a good guard dog, so I wasn't worried about any mountain lions or bears wandering into our makeshift camp.

We had no matches, so I opted for the fire plow method of fire-starting. I found a long, dry stick about as wide as my fist. Breaking it in half, I took the end that was about three feet long. There was a split in one half and by using a stone as a wedge I halved it like stringed cheese.

Wedging the curved side into the dirt to secure it, I kept the newly exposed inside face up. With the sharp edge of the other half, I began plowing a furrow in the other piece.

Smoke began to rise from the friction and the stick began to blacken around the path of travel. It was painstaking work and soon I was sweating profusely. My hands were well-calloused, but I could feel the potential for blisters breaking out on my hands.

The channel I was carving got deeper and was hot to the touch. Smoke continued to emanate from the furrow and when Kami carefully added the driest and smallest of the kindling, we got a small blaze going with the hot dust in the groove.

It wasn't much, but it was comforting. Kaytee led us in prayer and after a small snack, they all drifted off, huddled together for warmth and a sense of security, like newborn puppies. Shadow paced around the edge of the firelight. He came up to me as if to report that all was well, and then curled up next to Olivia, who was on the edge of the pack.

I sat on the opposite side of the fire, idly nudging the coals with a thin branch, my back against an old tree.

Looking up as the smoke filtered through the low boughs, I could see a smattering of stars. None of them shooting.

I wanted to stay awake. I wanted to keep watch.

But my eyelids drooped, and my head nodded as sleep stole over me. The fire was burning low, and I could smell the smoke, the pine, and the earth. I felt the pain of days and the bumps and bruises that peppered me from head to toe. I took a long deep breath and slowly blew it out.

I reached out in my mind, in my heart, and in my prayers for Melanie. It was unconscionable that I had let her fall into their hands, but I didn't know what else I could have done.

No matter. An almost palpable resolve rose from deep within me. I would rescue her.

I wasn't sure when I finally drifted off, but I knew that I was dreaming. I was standing in the sky above the mountains as though on top of an invisible bridge. The stars surrounded me on every side both above and below.

The shooting star we had seen on our first night appeared again, arcing by. It glowed with a pale green light. A single mountain peak jutted high above the rest, and the comet struck it with a flashing impact. All around the crater burst into flame. The forest caught fire and the whole mountainside burned green and then, standing before me in the sky was Tobar. He was encompassed by green flames as well. He held his tomahawk and pointed it at me.

"Do you dream often, Sawyer?" he asked in his hollow, cavernous voice.

"Now and then." Tentatively, I stepped forward and though there was nothing below me, I did not plummet down to earth but stayed level with him.

"Why not dream forever?" He ran a thumb along the edge of the blade.

We were standing still but the stars and the smoke and the flames all around us began to spin, slowly at first, but faster and faster until it was a blur.

Seemingly of its own accord, the charm around Tobar's neck began to sway as well, bouncing and swinging in a crazy dance.

It was hypnotizing.

Tobar suddenly threw the flaming tomahawk, and it spun like the blades on a windmill. Straight towards my face.

The tomahawk struck but I felt no pain.

Suddenly, I fell.

I knew I was only dreaming.

But I was still falling.

Then, with a start and quick intake of breath, I sat up.

And felt the barrel of a gun, pressed hard against the back of my head.

CHAPTER FOURTEEN

I blinked myself awake and gritted my teeth, hardly believing that I had allowed them to sneak up on me.

Again.

You're slipping, Sawyer, I mentally chided myself.

It is an important skill to be able to suppress the knee-jerk reaction to shout or scream or exclaim when you happen to be surprised.

I stayed silent.

Where was Shadow? Surely, he would have heard or smelled any approaching hostiles.

Slowly, I raised my hands.

Then an unfamiliar and distinctly feminine voice whispered harshly. "Easy, mister, you just go right on settin' there or I'll give you both barrels of this here shotgun."

A lot of people start talking, and often that can be a workable solution, at least temporarily, to buy time, establish rapport, distract, deescalate, or whatever.

But I said nothing.

The girls hadn't stirred. The fire had burned down to glowing coals.

No sign of Shadow.

"Where is the rest of your outfit?" the stranger asked.

Still not moving, I said slowly back to her, "I'm not one of them. I am a friend to these kids. I am trying to rescue them."

She pressed the bore of the shotgun tighter against the back of my head.

"Ask them." I said.

"Oh, I intend to."

Then, from the inky blackness behind us came a low growl.

I felt a single, ever-so-slight tremor ripple down through the barrel. Not enough to be fear, but perhaps just a bit of surprise.

"Mister, is that your dog?"

"Yep."

"You want to call him off?"

"I don't know. Do I? Maybe if you set down your weapon we can talk."

The pressure released from the back of my head.

"You can shoot me all you want but don't shoot my dog." I said.

I exhaled as she withdrew the shotgun from the back of my skull and then heard her step back and lean the gun against the back of the tree. I snapped my fingers and called for Shadow to come.

Shadow approached until he was standing next to me and looking up at the woman as she moved to where I could see her.

She was dressed for the weather, sturdy well-worn boots, rip-stop pants, and a layered and pocketed shirt. She had on a battered cowboy hat and an open riding coat. A large and lethal-looking Bowie knife hung from her belt. She stood there for a moment, lithe, capable, and sure of herself.

Squatting down on her heels, she held out a hand for Shadow, who, after a moment, sniffed and licked at her fingers.

Lowering herself to the ground, she drew her knees up and wrapped her hands around them.

She looked at me and spoke softly. "Dogs are good judges of character. I have seen this one a'fore but never this close. Sure is a big brute."

Shadow law down and sighed heavily out of his nose, illustrating the dissipation of the tension that had hung so heavy just moments before.

"Who are you?" I asked.

"Name's Lark."

"Like the bird?"

"Birds" She said, emphasizing the *s*. "Nearly a hundred different kinds of larks in the world. Only two here in California, though."

I nodded. "Ground-dwelling birds with beautiful songs. I've heard of them."

She chuckled. "Ground-dweller, that's me alright but it's been quite a spell since I sung a tune."

"Well, don't start now." I said, inclining my head to the sleeping teens.

She smiled but then her eyes seemed to sharpen. "You mind telling me what you and all these girls are doing running around my woods getting chased by Mexicans?"

She said it *Messicans.*

"Your woods?"

"That's right." She said. "*My* woods."

I told her about the camp and the kidnapping and about Shadow, the river, and the logjam. She listened patiently, not asking any questions until I had finished.

"So, your gal, this Melanie, is still with those hombres, headed to who knows where?"

"Yep, and I have got to get her back. Look, Lark, I know you don't know me, and you don't owe me anything, but will you help us?"

She looked at me, and then at each of the girls. Then she looked at Shadow. His ears twitched and he looked back at her, lilting his head to one side. I wondered if she could carry on the same kind of silent conversations with him that I did.

Looking back at me she gave me a nod and was on her feet in a single, fluid motion. She retrieved her over-under shotgun. I did not recognize the model but respected the obvious wear and care of the weapon. Casually, she swung the business end in my direction for a second and I got a perfect look down the twin barrels staring back at me like the eyeless sockets in a sideways skull.

My gaze lifted to Lark's face, and she gave me a fierce but pleasant smile. She tilted her head to watch me in a way that was somewhat bird-like but instead of reminding me of the songbird with which she shared a name, I could only see a proud bird of prey.

I roused the kids and we set off following Lark. She was an expert woodsman. *Woodswoman.* She never took a misstep, never crunched a twig, all the while making it look effortless. Shadow moved up and down the line, panting contentedly. The girls were panting too, but not so contentedly. It was all we could do, and sometimes beyond what we could do, to keep pace with our new guide.

Shadow moved ahead of our procession, loping along next to Lark.

Whenever we fell too far behind, Lark and Shadow simply stopped and waited for us to catch up.

Gray pre-dawn light began to tinge the forest and I was just about to ask for a breather for the girls when thirty yards ahead of us, Lark and Shadow stopped.

The trees thinned and before us we saw a steep rise of rock outcropping that rose up into knuckled ridges. There was scrub brush and scraggly trees dotting the slopes like pock marks.

I motioned the girls to sit as I walked ahead to Lark, squatting down to pet Shadow.

"Lark, we're not going to be able to climb that. Not without a rest."

"We ain't going over, we're going through." With that pronouncement, she pulled a clump of juniper back to reveal a narrow fissure in the rock. It was concealed not only by the foliage but also by the angle of the rock wall so that the cavity could have been easily mistaken for nothing more than a fold in the rock.

Lark slipped inside, leaving me to hold back the juniper. After a beat I motioned for the girls to follow. Shadow waited for the girls to line up and lead them through.

Beyond the entrance the passage widened but not by much. It was low-ceilinged and at some points both my shoulders scraped the sides. We could see the literal light at the end of the tunnel, not more than two-hundred feet away on a gentle upward slope. Shadow padded along ahead of us.

I was relieved that no matter how strong Tobar was, there was no way he could fit through here, even if he could find it.

The cave opened up to a wide, flat area about the size of two football fields full of straight and tall trees. The steep ridges and cliffs seemed to converge into a conical form around us as though we were inside a volcano. There were many rocks strewn about, all in varying sizes. There was a small lake, or maybe a large pond depending on how you classify things, situated on the opposite side of the enclosed area.

Shadow ran ahead to sit next to Lark, who stood fifty yards away, looking up at the sky.

"I'm surprised you didn't blindfold us." I said only half kidding to Lark. "You've got your own little impregnable Eden here."

She waved my remark off. "You couldn't find this place again in a hundred years. This place here is in a long narrow canyon and can't be seen unless you're right up there on the rim, maybe not even then."

"Come on." Lark said and led us to the front door of a sturdy log cabin around which was a series of makeshift planter boxes with all manner of vegetables growing.

The cabin was a single-roomed, sturdy structure. While not spacious, especially with all of us, it was remarkably comfortable and full of things that made it feel both homey and fortified.

There were assorted cast iron pans and copper pots hanging above the small wood stove. There were several faded framed photographs, rugs, and blankets and dogeared Lucy Maud Montgomery and Louisa May Alcott paperbacks. A bouquet of wheat hung above the bed. In the center of the rough table was a big jar full of dried cayenne peppers, so bright and red they seemed to glow like the coals in a hearth. A hand-painted, life-sized ceramic squirrel statue sat on the window still. It had one tiny chip on its nose that gave it a somewhat shabby, endearing look. He reminded me of me.

What was even better than the décor was the veritable arsenal she had on display. There were several long guns as well as pistols positioned strategically throughout the cabin so that no matter where she stood, a firearm was within easy reach. I noted a lever action 30-30 and .22 rifle, another shotgun, a more modern carbine with a long magazine, several revolvers, and Colt 1911 with antler grips. There were a series of knives from classic Bowies to KBARs, but what was the most anachronistic of armaments was a dusty Japanese sword that rested blade up above the fireplace.

As a teenager, I had been fascinated with the art of Bushido, the honor code of the samurai, like the code of Chivalry among European knights. My big brother had lived in Japan for several years and had married a girl from there. We had trained with the bamboo kendo swords and bokkens, the wooden katanas, extensively.

While not a proper katana, this sword of Lark's looked like the *gunto* used famously in the second World War.

The girls were also enamored with furnishings, oohing and aahing at the knick-knacks.

Lark leaned her current weapon of choice next to the door. She pointed me to an old canteen with US ARMY stenciled on the canvas sleeve that stood on the table. I opened the lid, sniffed and drank. It was cold and clear water, with just a hint of the metallic taste. I passed it around and the girls drank deeply and soon stretched out anywhere they could.

Taylor looked at me sleepily, but like she wanted to stay alert. "Are we safe here, Sawyer?"

I nodded and Shadow moved to her for a scratch behind the ear.

Satisfied, Taylor lay down and soon each of the girls were sleeping again, more soundly than they had in the woods.

"Aren't you going to ask me what in the world I am doing out here?" Lark said softly.

I shrugged, "I figured if you felt like sharing that you would have already. I got the idea that you kind of like to be left alone."

She smiled and started preparing food as quietly as she could.

Shadow slipped out the door that was still slightly ajar and trotted to the side of the lake for a drink.

"Make yourself useful and fetch some fish for the fry pan. There's a collapsible fishing rod and a filet knife in that there footlocker."

"Lark, I know I'm asking a lot, but I've got to go and get Melanie. She's in danger, and every minute she gets further and further away."

"Not until you've eaten something. You need a mite of rest, too. I know where they're going. Why, I've seen those hombres before, at least the big one you described. I've seen him and others like him crawling all over these mountains from time to time. They're as mean as rattlesnakes with toothaches and much more poisonous. Now I'm skeptical of spooks and haunts and the like of other worlds—I much prefer my own world—but this is a strange and wild country. Not all things that go bump in the night wait until it's necessarily nighttime. I've walked these mountains and woods alone for a long time, and sometimes I've felt watched. Sometimes I did the watching. That big beast, Tobar, I seen him and his ilk in their strange ceremonies, always in the same place. At the top of the waterfall."

"What do they do?"

"Can't rightly say. I never got too close, but they never had a prisoner before as far as I can tell."

"Where can I find this waterfall?"

"If you wanted to go overland, that'd back the way we came, but there's a short cut underground."

"Will you show me the way?"

She looked at me for a moment without speaking. "I reckon if you're bound and determined to go running off without a proper plan of action then I can't stop you.

You just go to the other side of the lake and beyond the trees you'll see several big boulders littered about. Right there is a cave. It is a long, dark way. I've only gone through there a couple of times and it's a tight squeeze, especially for a well-fed, broad-shouldered boy like yourself, but you just keep on going. It's a long way and longer than it seems what with the dark and all. I can lend you a lantern. The tunnel lets out no more than three miles to the waterfall itself."

"Can you take care of these girls? Make sure they get back to the camp? I'm sure everyone from the park service to the National Guard has been called in."

She folded her arms and leaned against the wall. "You're mighty trusting of a well-heeled stranger living out in the woods."

I pointed to her books. "Anyone who reads *Anne of Green Gables* and *Little Women* can't be all bad."

Then a thought occurred to me. I produced my copy of the Book of Mormon.

"Here, this is the best thing I can give you in exchange for your help."

She took it and I could see a light in her eyes.

"Thanks, son, it's hard to find good books this high up in the mountains."

"It's the best book."

"Well, if you're gonna go, you better go." she said, moving to the door.

"One more thing, can I borrow that sword?"

She glanced at the blade and then back to me. "That's been in my family for quite a spell, son, that's a lot to ask. You gonna put it to good use?"

"I hope I won't have to."

"You want a gun instead?"

I shook my head. "Not my style."

She sighed. "Suit yourself, that one is mostly just for decoration, but it's still sharp."

She took it down and handed it to me. From a pack she fished out a flashlight and tossed it to me.

I clicked it on and off, checking its strength.

"Batteries are fresh." She said.

"Thank you." Looking around at the girls, I said, "Please make sure they're okay."

She shooed me out, "You just get that gal of yours back in one piece."

Slipping out the door, I stepped down into the dawn, drawing the sword and looking along the edge.

I slashed it through the air back and forth, testing the weight. I twirled it expertly in a figure-eight, and with the symbolic blood flick, returned it to its sheath.

"Seems to be in tune and looks like you know how to play it." Lark said from behind me. I hadn't heard her approach "If it were me, I'd use it. Kill 'em, kill 'em all. Every last murdering one of 'em."

I nodded, said nothing, because I wasn't sure how to respond. I wasn't sure if I was ready to kill anyone.

To be killed, yes. I was beyond prepared for that possibility. Just so long as Melanie and the girls were out of harm's way, it didn't matter what happened to me.

Grasping the sword in my left and the flashlight in my right, I set off running for the far side of the lake.

Shadow, his muzzle dripping with water, appeared at my side. His big, dark eyes seemed to say, *what took you so long?*

I stopped and held my hand out. "Not this time, boy. Stay. I need you to watch the girls."

He slowed to a halt and closed his mouth, turning his head quizzically.

"Go on, boy, and don't let Lark mistake you for a polar bear. She might shoot you."

CHAPTER FIFTEEN

I found the scattered granite boulders, laid out as though they had been thrown from the peaks by some monster long ago in a game of primeval Bacchi ball.

The mouth of the cave yawned before me like a maw full of jagged, broken teeth. It was still early and getting lighter out but nevertheless I hit the black portal with the flashlight's beam.

No effect.

It might have been the budding sunlight or the low level of lumens, but the cavern's hollow eye socket proved impenetrable and impervious to light. Picking up a small stone, I tossed it to test the depth. It was immediately swallowed from sight as if it had vanished by magic. But I heard it clatter around and knew it was not a sudden drop off.

Stepping beyond the threshold, I felt the palpable difference in temperature. Not as cold as opening a walk-in freezer but as distinct as when you are in the shower and the hot water starts running low.

I took a minute for my eyes to adjust to the gloom. Playing my flashlight over the ribs of the rocky cave, I was impressed by the size of it. It hadn't appeared so vast from the outside, but I could see that an entire cathedral could be crammed inside.

The dark didn't worry me. Not with the flashlight. Lark had explored these earthen halls and had emerged unscathed. I would do the same.

She was much smaller than me though, and I didn't have a handy gadget to combat confined spaces. Though the tunnel that extended past the vast entryway looked large—about fifteen or twenty feet high and almost as much across. Big enough, for now.

I walked on, my senses straining to calibrate. My vision was reduced to the reach of my flashlight, all I could touch, and smell was the damp stone, which I was disinclined to taste. Some sounds were of course muted by being underground and yet some seemed strangely amplified. Weird subterranean acoustics.

Using the sword as a makeshift walking stick, I scraped my way along. Looking back, I was surprised to see how small the aperture of light at the opening had become. Just a small spot of sunlight against the implacable darkness. Soon, I rounded a corner and the way from which I had come was completely lost to sight.

I don't wear a watch. I can usually approximate the time by the sun or my own internal sense of chronology but underground I lost all sense of the passage of time.

Had it been five minutes or an hour? So many caves in our country have been explored and there is often evidence of spelunkers or even the detritus and graffiti of vandals left behind in perhaps an unconscious homage to ancient cave paintings. But there was nothing in this tunnel. And as much as I loathe litter, it might have been a comfort to know that people had frequented this site before.

My sense of adventure was outweighed by my concern for Melanie. The girls, I felt sure, were well-cared for in the hands of Lark and the paws of Shadow. But why was I so worried?

Are we not all well-cared for in the hands of God?

Of course, but I know faith to be a principle of action and while God is the conductor on the train of eternity, I at least have to shovel coal.

Coal.

I thought of the coal mines and the canaries and how many people had been trapped in collapses and cave-ins.

I think it was Jane Austen who wrote, "what are men to rocks and mountains?"

I didn't have an answer, but the rocks and mountains had better get used to me because I was coming through.

Or perhaps they didn't notice that I was there at all.

It was even cooler now and I was glad that I had my sweater, even though it was still slightly damp. But my movement helped to keep me warm enough. The ceiling lowered and the walls closed in at times only to widen again further ahead.

It was as though the entire cave had been made from a giant accordion. In some places expanded and others contracted.

The path dipped, ran straight, and rose steeply at times. After a series of ups and downs, I climbed up a particularly steep incline. It reminded me of my childhood days and scrambling up the playground slides the wrong way.

Reaching the top, I sat on the peak and swung my legs around to scoot down the opposite slope. It was markedly steeper, and I slid faster than expected. Loose rocks fell around me.

I hit the ground running and stumbling. My flashlight beam waved around crazily as I pumped my arms.

I failed to notice the lowered ceiling and collided headfirst with the rock shelf.

In all my boxing matches and street fights, I have never been knocked out. I didn't see stars so much as felt them circling like in a cartoon. The lights might have been on upstairs, but I was decidedly not at home. My knees gave out first, the lights flickered, and then it was a domino effect from there until I sank to the floor.

Asleep.
Out cold.
Dead to the world.

I was back in Lark's cabin. It was dark but a fire crackled cozily in the hearth. No one else was inside. I couldn't see the moon or the stars through the windows—couldn't see anything at all. It was as though someone had painted the panes matte black.

Moving about the cabin, I came to the door. Checked it and, hesitating a moment, dropped the bar into place.

As soon as I stepped back, I sensed a huge presence on the other side of the door. There was a creak and a crack as whatever was on the other side pressed its considerable weight against the door. The heavy bar bowed, and the timbers groaned, and the hinges moaned but still it held.

I waited with bated breath.

I should have kept breathing.

With a bone-rattling crash, the door burst inward followed by a wall of water. In seconds, the flood was over my head and the ceiling was gone, as was the night.

From high above beams of daylight drifted down in kaleidoscopic patterns. Suddenly, Melanie was beside me. My air was quickly running out, but she grabbed my face and pressed her lips to mine in a tight seal, breathing into me.

Then, with the grace of a mermaid, she fluttered-kicked up and away.

I tried to follow, but I felt leaden. Looking up through the bubbly water, I saw a body sinking towards me. Fearful for Melanie, I reached out only to see that the lifeless form was me. A tomahawk buried in my heart. Thin tendrils of blood ribboned out of the wound and a huge shadow passed over me.

There was a blur of bubbles and all I saw was a wide mouth full of rows of serrated razor teeth.

I sat bold upright and nearly hit my head again. It was black as pitch, but I could sense the lump on my forehead almost touching the stone shelf I had struck. My eyes strained to absorb just an ounce of light but there was nothing. Gingerly, I felt my forehead and the tender goose egg. No blood though. Behind me was the way I had come and before me was where the rock overhang made a space just big enough for me to move on all fours.

Being in absolute darkness is nothing like being in a dark room, or closet. There is usually some adjacent illumination, like from a streetlamp, the moon, or a hall light left on making a golden sliver at the base of the door.

I'm not afraid of the dark, but I felt an encroachment of claustrophobia that I had never experienced before. I felt around further into the space ahead of me as well as behind, looking for my flashlight and sword. Trying to breathe evenly.

One of my mission companions had been an underwater welder in Peru and he had taught me a breathing exercise. In for four seconds and out for four seconds, repeated four times.

It helped, a little.

I patted around and finally found the flashlight.

Broken.

Or the batteries had not been as fresh as Lark had hoped.

Which made me wonder how long I had been out for.

I didn't stop fiddling with the flashlight until I was sure that it was beyond repair, at least by me and in the dark. Casting it away, I heard it crack against the stone wall.

Now there was some litter.

Sinking to my knees, I felt the crushing darkness wrap its leathery wings around me. I was reminded of the third book of Nephi, chapter ten, when after Christ's crucifixion in the Holy

Land, the people in the Americas were beset by thick darkness, darkness that was so strong that no lights could be kindled.

I couldn't go back, and I couldn't go forward. I felt doomed to languish in the strangling dark until hunger and thirst destroyed me.

I closed my eyes—not that it made any difference.

Then I prayed.

I prayed for a long time.

I don't remember all the words, but I needed help and, more than that, I needed to be of help to Melanie and if I were consigned to die in a deep dark cave, then so be it. But it would have to wait until Melanie and the girls were well out of harm's way.

I closed my prayer and began to sing my favorite hymn, one that had carried me through tough times as a missionary.

> *Abide with me! fast falls the eventide;*
> *The darkness deepens. Lord, with me abide!*
> *When other helpers fail and comforts flee,*
> *Help of the helpless, oh, abide with me!*

My voice sounded far away. I never was particularly good at singing, but I kept going, standing up with the second verse.

> *Swift to its close ebbs out life's little day.*
> *Earth's joys grow dim; its glories pass away.*
> *Change and decay in all around I see;*
> *O thou who changest not, abide with me!*

Resting my hand against the outcropping of rock that I had run into, my foot kicked against something—the sword! Still singing, I picked it up.

> *I need thy presence ev'ry passing hour.*
> *What but thy grace can foil the tempter's pow'r?*

Who, like thyself, my guide and stay can be?
Thru cloud and sunshine, Lord, abide with me!

With a sword in hand and a song in my heart, I was filled with new hope. Men had conquered nations with nothing more than a sword. I sang some more, the same song, but this time in Spanish.

Ven, oh Señor; la noche viene ya.
Todo es oscuro y temor me da.
No hay amparo; gran maldad se ve.
En las tinieblas acompáñame.
Veloz se va la vida con su afán.
Su gloria, sus ensueños pasarán.
Gran decadencia por doquier se ve.
Ven, oh Señor, y acompáñame.
Siempre Tu gracia quiero yo tener.
¿Quién más podrá a Satanás vencer?
Sólo en Ti mi guía hallaré.
En sol y sombra, acompáñame.

Breathing steadily, I bent down and began to crawl under the rock shelf, keeping the sword out in front of me to feel for any sudden drops or dead ends. The ceiling scraped against my back in places as I moved slowly on my knees.

For several yards I had to go down onto my belly and was just beginning to think that the passage would become too narrow for me when the floor sloped down and the ceiling opened up.

Using the sword like a blind man's cane, I tapped and reached all around. Once I was sure I could stand without hitting my head, I rose up. The walls were smoother here and more damp. I could no longer touch the ceiling. Feeling further along the wall, I discovered a narrow fissure that seemed to be the only way onward.

I had to turn sideways to scoot through and I realized that burgers more than once a week would have made it impassable for me. After an uncomfortable few yards, I found myself again in a wide chamber. Running my hands along the wall until I had made a circuit and returned to the fissure I had just come from. At least, I thought it was where I had come from. It was hard to tell in the complete dark. I decided to explore the center of the room.

Searching about with the sword, I felt something loose. Not rock. Reaching down I felt something lighter and thin and solid and smooth. For a half-second I thought, *bones*.

Then I realized they were sticks, some peeled, some with bark in places. All in a neat pile. A campfire? Could I find a lighter or some matches? Carefully, in ever-widening circles, I felt around the sticks for anything else. On my third revolution, I found a small stone with sharp edges that fit neatly in the palm of my hand.

Hoping against hope that it could be flint, I drew the steel sword and struck the stone and the spine of the blade together.

A spark.

And something else.

CHAPTER SIXTEEN

Shadows.

Immense, sharp shadows, reached up like knives in the dark. Then they were gone, and I was once again blind.

I found the pile of sticks and what felt like very, very dry moss. I had to strike the flint and steel three more times before the kindling caught. The shadows returned with each attempt like overseers who were meant to check on my progress and were likely unimpressed.

I broke some sticks and blew gently, and steadily into the bed of moss. I smelled what little smoke came up and watched the glow brighten and dim with each breath.

The splintered sticks blackened at the broken edges, smoldered, and burned. The shadows grew at a commensurate rate with the light of the fire.

It was painstaking to nurse my fire into a blaze but the light, even the early glow, had been a supreme source of reassurance. Now, though, the shadows filled me with foreboding. They were unnatural. Spectral. Unlike those we grow up playing puppet games with on our bedroom walls. These moved irregularly, not quite in rhythm with the flickering fire. They swayed like seaweed, hemming me in and moving furtively, like actual creatures around the edge of a campfire. I watched them, mesmerized, as if by the undulations of a king cobra.

I considered extinguishing the fire. They couldn't live without it. They would die in the dark. I raised my foot to stamp out the blaze and felt my arms prickle with goosebumps. If the fire went out, then there would be nothing but shadow.

I didn't want to be in the dark. The shadows seemed to sense my predicament. Like being between a rock and a hard place, or as the French say, between the hammer and the anvil. Or better yet, in Latin, *a fronte praecipitium, a tergo lupi,* meaning a precipice in front, wolves behind.

I licked my dry lips and watched the shadows swell. They were on a two-dimensional plane but seemed to pass into a third. Some moved, others seemed to stand still.

I felt waves of icy fear ripple through me, and I was rooted to the spot. I thought of piling more fuel on the fire, perhaps to shrink the shadows. But then the fire would die all the sooner and I would be left to the dark.

The shadows relished my indecision and shook with silent laughter.

My sword, still drawn, turned in my hand, reflecting the firelight. I pointed the tip of my blade at each of the shadows in turn.

To no avail.

I couldn't fight darkness with mere force. I sat down. Looking for some warmth but the fire did little to lessen the coolness of the cave. I looked for my own shadow to fight the disembodied shadows. There were too many, though. The ones cast by the fire were now discernible as I watched, but the others that were out of sync seemed to multiply. Some were broad and short, others tall and thin. They danced menacingly.

The hair on the back of my neck was as prickly as a porcupine and my skin crawled. I looked into the fire, inadvisable because it spoils your dark vision, but I dared not look at the shadows. And yet I couldn't look away. I glanced back and forth from fire to shadow.

"I am not afraid of you." I said aloud. My voice sounded small, and the faint and fading echoes somehow made it smaller. "You can't hurt me." I tried again.

No reaction.

I put a few more sticks on the fire. I stood up again and the shadows grew larger.

"I'm on an important mission and I don't have time for superstitions and shadows. You have nothing to do with me either so if you will show me the way out, I'll be on my way."

The firelight shadows flickered quickly but the others slowed down, almost standing still. I felt a breath of air. Taking up a stick from the fire, I looked along the wall for the source of the draft. I couldn't see anything but dark rock. And then I saw an even darker line, slanted, jagged, extending from floor to ceiling. I stepped nearer and discerned a cleft in the wall formed by two overlapping sections of rock. I was sure it had not been there when I first entered the room. I looked back at the firelight and the shadows.

"Thank you." I said.

With sword in one hand and stick in the other, I slipped into the crevice and kept moving forward. The draft made my firebrand flare up and though it wasn't very bright, it was a night and day difference from journeying in the dark.

Suddenly, I heard a voice. Sighing like wind in the tunnels. Whether in my mind or ears I couldn't be sure.

"Find her." It said.

I looked back, but a dogleg in the path obscured my view of the room I had just left. I couldn't even see signs of the firelight anymore.

"I will." I said back.

There was a short but steep rise, and I felt the temperature change. My quasi-torch had gone out but now I could see a scrap of sky ahead. It was deep, velvety blue and full of stars.

Nighttime.

I had been in the cave all day, at least.

I gulped down deep breaths of the cool mountain air, hardly daring to believe I was free from the darkness of the tunnels. I let my eyes focus far, trying to make out the shapes of the mountains against the night but I was at a completely different angle and saw no discernible landmarks other than the ribbon of river shining white from the moon and starlight.

I heard crickets.

A good sound.

I started winding my way down the mountain in between trees. It was slow going in the dark, but I felt much better above ground, nighttime or not.

It never crossed my mind that I might never find Melanie. We were in the trackless wilderness. Thousands upon thousands of square miles over rugged terrain.

No matter.

Come hell or high water I was going to get her back. And both high water and hell had already come as far as I was concerned.

The river, while not especially deep, had been high enough and though not burgeoning with brimstone, the underdark had been beyond hellish.

Nothing else could stand in my way.

I heard furtive sounds in the undergrowth. Little critters scurrying to their dens. The hoot of a great horned owl.

Perhaps two, talking to one another.

Something larger moved away from me deeper into the brush but I couldn't guess what it was. An elk, maybe.

After a steady descent, the ground leveled out and I found a more well-worn trail.

Lark had said that the waterfall was only a few miles from the cave exit, but I couldn't hear the familiar rushing and couldn't even see the river anymore. Maybe I would have to wait until daylight to find my way.

The path grew sandy and cut along a rocky cliff and I finally spotted the river a couple hundred feet away. Then I noticed something else.

Firelight.

Only for a second, since I was still walking. I stepped back, too far and couldn't see it. Maybe it had just been my imagination. A trick of the light.

I bobbed and weaved my head around, trying to find the right angle.

There! I saw it again.

It was hard to judge the distance, but it couldn't have been more than a quarter mile away.

I started for it.

My sword at the ready.

Ready for what, I didn't know.

If I had been smart, I would have gone in swinging. No questions asked. Just cutting down my enemies before they could stand.

But I had never killed before and didn't want to start then. I judged the reverse edge of the blade. Dull but solid.

Maybe just the threat of violence would be enough for these people. That seemed to be their preferred mode of operation.

Threatening their victims with violence.

Let's see how they liked the taste of their own medicine.

Most people have never been shot before. It is something they've thought about but only in the abstract. It is all theoretical. Just Hollywood.

But almost everyone has been cut at one point or another. Whether by paper, a pocket or kitchen knife, a bit of broken glass. Even a safety razor while shaving. And cuts, even minor ones, can bleed a lot. There is something that instills an ancient fear of cold steel. Something that still remembers the barbarian hordes and the brigands. The pirates and the Vikings. Or in my case, the Samurai.

Even Tobar seemed to understand this principle in his use of a comparatively crude weapon. He would have been somehow less intimidating with a firearm. Not that there were many trigger guards in the world that would fit his finger.

I gripped my sword tight.

I could hear low voices.

Spanish.

I crept closer, trying to make out the words.

It was Lugo and Soto.

They were sitting, hunched slightly, extending their hands to the fire. Their guns rested against the trunks of trees maybe a yard behind them. Within easy reach. But not too easy.

A swing of the sword would be faster than they could bring their guns to bear.

But I didn't want to kill them, not yet.

I crept around the clearing until I was behind them. I tried to avoid brittle branches or leaves, anything that would make a sound. But my boots were not moccasins. Lugo and Soto must have heard or sensed something because they turned just in time to see me lunge from the darkness.

The firelight glinted off my sword as I menaced them with the blade. Reeling back in surprise and fear, they nearly fell into the fire, fumbling in a rush for their rifles.

Suddenly they stopped and seemed *relieved.*

"Sawyer." Soto said. "You nearly gave me a heart attack." He patted his chest to give emphasis and gave a long exhalation.

Lugo wiped his brow and smiled at me. "We thought you were Tobar."

Well, I just stood there, my sword still poised at the ready. Was this a ruse? A trap to lull me into a false sense of security? I hadn't felt secure in quite a while, falsely or otherwise.

I must have had an incredulous expression on my face because they both exchanged a look and turned back to me, almost apologetically.

"Forgive us, Sawyer, so much has happened since the river. Won't you sit down?"

I shook my head, not only in answer to his invitation but also to make sure I was seeing and hearing them right.

"Where's Melanie?" I growled.

"I'm right here, Sawyer."

I turned and saw her standing there, as lovely as ever. I couldn't say she was the girl of my dreams because I had never ever dreamed so good.

Her hair was a mess, and her clothes were torn and dirty. She had an armful of firewood, but she dropped it when our eyes met.

I shoved my sword into the ground, stepping forward to embrace her. I couldn't say whose grip was stronger. I would have been happy to have never let go and just stand there until the end of the world.

"The girls?" she said breathlessly.

"They're safe." Remembering Lugo and Soto, I turned, still holding Melanie around the shoulders with one arm. "What's with Heckle and Jeckle?"

"Hey!" Lugo said, sounding genuinely hurt.

Soto puffed out his chest. "We're the good guys now."

I glanced at Melanie in consternation. She raised an eyebrow back at me and gestured to them.

"Well?" I said.

Soto cleared his throat. "At the river, when Melanie saved you all, I—I remembered when I was a boy. I was playing on a dock. I fell in and a girl from the village jumped in after me. Neither of us could swim but she was just tall enough to hold me above water. Someone came in time for me, but she drowned." He trailed off, gazing into the fire.

I pursed my lips, and let the gravity of his story sink in. Then I lifted my chin towards Lugo. "What about you?"

He shrugged. "You and Melanie saved Soto's life. You and Melanie spared our lives in Tijuana. I have nieces. I don't want to do this anymore."

"Somehow, I don't think Tobar shares your contrition. Where is he?"

"I shot him." Soto said.

A jolt of electricity sparked through me.

My mortal enemy. Dead.

Melanie gently slipped out from under my arm and stood by Soto and Lugo. "It's true, Sawyer, they saved me."

I looked at the three of them. "You saw his body?"

Lugo shook his head. "Soto got him, in the back. He fell over a cliff."

CHAPTER SEVENTEEN

Tobar was dead.

The thought gave me a shock of relief. Not that I didn't retain a sense of having been cheated out of a final showdown with a formidable enemy, but hubris has been the downfall of greater men than me from Achilles to Custer.

At any rate, I wasn't even sure that I could have beaten Tobar one on one even with a sword.

I turned to Lugo. "But when I showed up you and Soto said that you thought I was Tobar."

"Well, yeah, I mean, you know, his *espíritu.* His spirit. He was a bad *hombre.*"

Soto chimed it, "not even a man. Not really."

"Where'd this happen?" I asked.

Soto gestured in the direction of the river. "Near *la catarata*, the waterfall."

"You saw it?" I asked Melanie.

The three of them hesitated. "I didn't see him get hit, but he disappeared over the edge."

Soto pressed, "I couldn't have missed, I'm sure."

Melanie put a hand on my chest. "Sawyer, you look dead on your feet, you need to rest."

Soto and Lugo agreed.

"Negative. We need to get back to the girls, pronto. Let's get moving."

Melanie's hand moved to my shoulder and squeezed gently but firmly. "Just close your eyes while we break camp."

I blinked. Realizing that I was running on empty, and we weren't even on the home stretch, not until we were all back together.

"Fine. Five minutes. No more. Just one of those power naps people are always talking about."

I was asleep before I remembered sitting down.

Moyobamba, San Martin, Peru: two years earlier

I shivered awake in my hammock.

Shivered?

In the jungle?

Geronimo was still sound asleep, swaying gently in his own hammock like a baby in a crib.

Moving to the window, I looked out into a world of white.

Thick mist hung low as far as I could see, which wasn't very far. Either we had ascended like the city of Enoch, unlikely, or there was a serious inversion.

It was well before our personal study time, so I let Geronimo sleep and did my morning routine. I did push-ups, prayer, brushed my teeth and sat down to study.

But I was still thinking about Brother Anibal. It had been more than a week since our visit to him.

The Bishop had confided that Anibal was awaiting trial and had been accused of the murder of an oil executive along with his wife and daughter. Anibal drove a mototaxi and the family had last been seen being driven by him. Anibal had admitted to chauffeuring them but couldn't say where they had gone after he had taken them to their destination. Blood had been found on the backseat of the mototaxi and no one else had seen the man or his family since.

I had been considering a career in law enforcement when I returned from my mission, but for now God's law was more my jurisdiction.

Still, I couldn't help but think that Anibal was innocent.

It was just a feeling, but a strong one.

Lost in thought, I glanced out the window again, and saw a figure materialize from the fog. He was stumbling and shuffling down the path.

Geronimo walked into the room, yawning. He moved to my side, looking to see what I was staring at, still rubbing sleep from his eyes. He was wrapped in one of the rough blankets that came standard issue to missionaries but which we had never needed to use.

He lip-pointed at the man tottering about. "Get a load of this *boracho.*"

There were a lot of drunks in Peru. I had seen them lying passed out in gutters or wandering city streets but somehow this guy was different.

He stopped in the middle of the street looking wide-eyed at nothing, then with a half-turn he teetered and fell face first into the dirt.

Snatching the blanket off Geronimo's shoulders, I ran out the front door.

"Hey!" He protested, slipping on a pair of sandals before following after me.

I ran to the man and got him into the recovery position, draping the blanket over him. He was chilled and yet sweaty. Like he was sick or something. He didn't stink of alcohol, but his eyes were bloodshot and out of focus.

I shook his shoulder, trying to elicit a response but got nothing.

"Sir, are you alright?" What happened?".

He tried to sit up, but he had hurt himself in the fall. His nose was bloodied, and pink bubbles gathered in the corners of his slightly open mouth.

I turned to Geronimo. "Go call the Bishop, he needs help."

I rubbed his back trying to warm him up and give him a bit of comfort and consolation. Medically he didn't look in imminent peril but underneath the blur of his eyes I sensed some sort of fear.

I looked him over again, trying to get some clues as to his identity. He was nicely dressed, if a little dirty. Designer white shirt and khakis. He was barefoot, which was odd. He had a wedding band on his finger and the tan line on his right wrist where a watch had been.

"Bishop is coming. He said he would call the police." Geronimo said, breathlessly.

Then it hit me.

I knew where this man's watch was, and I knew where his shoes were.

I knew who he was.

Moments later, the Bishop appeared and between the three of us we were able to get the man into our home.

"How did this man come to be here, Elders?"

"Bishop, where is Kucera?" I asked.

He was confused by my non sequitur.

"He, um, just left to visit Brother Anibal in the jail."

Without a word I ran outside. Dutifully, Geronimo followed. He was a great companion.

He was still in sandals but made a valiant effort to keep up with me. We were soon close enough to the main roads to flag down a mototaxi.

"It's an emergency." I told him.

He wasn't impressed. "Are you going to pay."

Exasperatedly, I almost yelled, "yes."

Geronimo and I piled onto the backseat, and I told him to hurry to the prison.

"Wait, what exactly are we doing?" Geronimo said over the whine of the motorcycle traversing the road at breakneck speed despite the low visibility.

"That man we found is the one Anibal was accused of killing. But I think Kucera and one of the guards at the prison are behind it."

"What are we going to do?"

"I haven't got that far." I said.

If Kucera was on foot, I figured that we might overtake him. What we would do then, I didn't know, but Anibal was in danger. If the guy had somehow escaped from them, then they would be looking to eliminate any potential witnesses. Their victim had apparently been drugged which is why we had taken him for drunk. But where were his wife and child?

The prison came into sight, and we hadn't caught up to Kucera.

No sooner had we disembarked from the mototaxi and handed him his *soles* than the earthquake struck.

"You have got to be kidding me." I said.

Sirens sounded and I was sure that the guards had a protocol for evacuating the inmates. If Kucera was there they would cut his visit short, but what about the other guard?

I ran through the main entrance with Geronimo on my heels. The power must have gone out in the tremor because only faint emergency bulbs burned over the exits, marking *SALIDA*.

There was no one at the intake desk.

No, there was *someone*, they were just slumped across the desk. One of the guards.

Dead?

Cautiously, I felt for a pulse.

He was alive.

In the dark, I gingerly searched for injuries and found his hair matted with blood from a hit to the head.

"Geronimo, you get him outside. I'll keep going."

He hesitated. We were not supposed to be apart, that was the mission, stick together.

Shouts and cries of terror sounded from the prisoners. The building still shook, and streams of dust sprinkled down on us.

"We got to hurry. This place could come down on us any second."

With a grunt of frustration, Geronimo took the guard under each armpit and began to drag him to the door.

I knew the way to Anibal's cell and moved along the hallway. It was like walking through hell.

I wanted to console the prisoners, tell them that I would get them out, but I couldn't risk Kucera catching wind of my presence.

I saw the beam of a flashlight click on and two figures stood before Anibal's door.

Kucera and his accomplice were speaking.

Edging closer, I could make out their words over the racket of the shaking building and the pleas sounding from the other cells.

"Did you kill the one at the front desk?" Kucera asked.

There was a second's pause and the guard replied. "Yes."

Anibal must have said something because Kucera kicked the door and cursed at him before turning to the guard.

"Open it."

Another second's hesitation.

"What are we going to do?"

"What must be done. No witnesses." Kucera hissed.

"This was just supposed to be for ransom, from the businessman. I am not going to kill anyone."

Kucera snatched the flashlight from the guard's grasp. For a second the light shone over me, but they must not have noticed. I froze momentarily before inching still closer. What I planned to do when I got to them, I had no idea.

"I thought you just said you killed your fellow officer."

The guard stammered a response, "I did, I just don't want to kill anyone more than we need to."

The building shook with renewed vigor and something came crashing down somewhere in the building.

"Give the keys to me." Kucera held out one of his talonlike hands.

I could only imagine Anibal's fear, listening to two men discussing his demise on the other side of a door only they could unlock.

The guard produced a ring of large keys.

"I've got it." He said and slowly fitted a key into the lock. Then he paused. I was almost on top of them, still unsure of my next move. "Tell me, what will happen to the woman and the child?"

Kucera rolled his eyes. "You fool, the man already escaped. Once we are done here, we will take what we need from them and go."

The guard turned the key but kept his hand on the door, holding it shut, hesitating. Perhaps what little conscience he had left was getting the better of him.

"Wait." I said.

They both turned in surprise. Kucera's face ugly with anger, the guard's masked in horror but perhaps a little hope that he didn't have to go through with this grim business.

"We found the man you had kidnapped. Only a matter of time before we get his family. The guard at the desk isn't dead. Neither of you are guilty of murder so you should quit while you are ahead."

The guard looked at Kucera, still holding the cell door shut. There was still no sound from inside but the building itself was straining. The walls were cracking.

"Sir," I said, "we need to get the rest of these inmates out. Right now."

"It's over." The guard said to Kucera.

I didn't think that anyone could have moved so fast. Kucera drew a machete from his belt and in the same motion severed the guard's right hand just above the wrist. The hand that had been holding the door.

The guard screamed and collapsed just as Anibal slammed the door open. It swung out and to the left, pinning Kucera against the wall where he dropped the flashlight.

Anibal held the door against him with all his strength, I ran to the guard who looked like he was going into shock. Scooping up the flashlight, I tried to get a good look at the scene before me. Tearing off the left sleeve of my white shirt, I used the cloth to staunch the bleeding.

Behind me, Anibal cried out. Kucera had gotten his weapon around and had slashed Anibal. It was a weak swing owing to the awkward angle, but it caused Anibal to lessen the pressure enough for Kucera to slip out from behind the cell door.

Using the flashlight, I shone the beam in his eyes. Wincing, he turned away long enough for me to hit him once, twice, three times with flashlight and fist. I caught his right wrist that held the machete in my left and using my considerable size advantage I hurled him bodily into the cell Anibal had just vacated.

I didn't know how long earthquakes lasted, or if this were some sort of aftershock or just the prison still reeling from the damage to its structural integrity but whatever the case, a fissure began to open in the floor of the cell.

Kucera screamed as the ground gave way beneath him and he fell.

Unsure of what came over me, I dove across to the widening hole and caught hold of Kucera's outstretched hand with my left. Bracing myself by holding onto a bit of newly exposed rebar.

"Hold on." I said, beginning to pull him up.

Some daylight trickled through a small grimy window in the cell, just enough for me to see Kucera. He looked frightened, just like a man who had almost fallen into a bottomless pit, but relieved that I had caught him.

As bad as he was, I wasn't going to let him die like that. He was much lighter than me and I was strong, but I wasn't sure I could pull him all the way up one-handed. Turning my head to call for Anibal's help, I caught something in the corner of my eye. A shadow seemed to pass across Kucera's face, and he turned hideous again. He still had the machete in his other hand and now he swung it right for me.

Instinctively, I let go.

He fell and the tip of the machete hit my left pinky finger, just along the knuckle.

I watched him fall, still staring back, until he was no longer visible. I didn't hear him hit the bottom and he never made a sound. I grit my teeth in pain, unsure if my finger was still attached.

Getting to my feet, I turned to Anibal and the guard.

"Let's go." I said, pressing my left hand under my right armpit.

The quake stopped and even though the prison was damaged badly, we were able to account for all the inmates. More police had shown up and medical personnel attended to the two guards.

My pinky finger was still serviceable, and I was excited at the prospect of a new scar. I had been told that chicks did in fact dig scars.

Geronimo and I were questioned for hours and by the end of it I was both hungry and tired. Pretty much the perpetual state of missionaries.

We would have to call the Mission President and let him know what had happened, but I figured that we should try and hit our numbers first. It wasn't a Preparation Day and we had yet to do much missionary work today.

We arrived back to town after dark. The town was in pitch darkness due to the power having gone out after the *terramoto*.

We walked aimlessly for a while until Geronimo stopped. "Why don't we just go home?" He said.

I kept walking and he caught up to me.

"The light will come back on soon."

"You think so?"

"Yes." I said.

At the exact moment that I said the word, the electricity surged back, and we were bathed in the welcome light.

Geronimo just looked at me incredulously.

"Wow, you must really have a lot of faith."

My eyes popped open, and I stood up. I didn't know how long I had been asleep for, but it felt like a lot more than five minutes.

"Hey, why didn't you wake me?" I asked Melanie.

"If you were too tired to set your internal alarm clock, then that meant you needed more sleep." She said. "Besides, it's only been a couple hours."

It was still dark out.

Extinguishing the fire, we set off in the direction I had come from. They had flashlights and foodstuffs which would make the journey easier.

I was still reticent to let them carry their weapons, but Melanie was sure of their sincerity, which was good enough for me.

Barely.

The thing about interrogations is that you always want to make it look like you know more than you do, and a lot more than they do. Then the trick is to get them to tell the rest of it to you.

"Did you know what Tobar was planning to do at the waterfall when this started?"

Lugo walked close behind me. "I mean, we knew that he had made pilgrimages here before, but this time was supposed to be different, you know. About the money. Tobar came because he knows these mountains."

"What about the other ones like Tobar?"

"Others?" Soto said. He sounded genuinely surprised. "I didn't think there were others like him, that there even could *be* others like him." He glanced around as if he half expected an army of tomahawk-wielding savages to swarm us.

I looked at Lugo. "You scared the kids with your stories about wendigos."

He looked sheepishly down at his shoes. "Just stories."

Melanie sipped from a water bottle and passed it to me. "Where did you hear about others?"

"An eye-witness account." Lugo and Soto might have taken great strides at making amends for their wicked ways, but I wasn't ready to trust them enough to reveal Lark's address, email, and social security number, so to speak.

I passed the water to Soto, looking him in the eye. "What's your plan once we get back?"

Soto drank and then Lugo. They looked at one another and then back at me.

"We don't know."

"Are you going to turn yourselves in?" I asked.

"I'm sure we can get you a deal." Melanie said. "You've helped us and can testify against your bosses."

"Or we can just let you go. Melanie is influential but she can't sway the Feds. Not much, anyway. So any plea bargain they cut you will almost certainly carry some jail time. Your former employers have a long memory and a longer reach. They could get to you in there. Something to think about."

We walked in silence for some time.

Melanie asked again and again how the girls were, and I reiterated that they were as safe as could be under the circumstances.

Pale gray light started to show, and the stars began to fade like little candles being extinguished one by one.

A thick mist rose far quicker than the sun and even though the light increased, our visibility did not improve.

Eventually, I stopped.

The mist was beginning to grow impenetrable. The sun was so shrouded that it looked like nothing more than a full moon and we could stare at it with impunity.

It was quiet.

Like the old Western cliché.

Too quiet.

Without warning there was the *ra-ta-tat-tat-tat* of gunfire from behind me. I whirled around and saw Lugo scanning the trees, his MP5K raised.

"Tobar!" Lugo said, not looking away from his sights. "I saw him."

Soto raised his own weapon, and I drew my sword. Melanie had taken cover behind the trunk of a tree, crouching, and looking around.

A large shadow appeared on the other side of the trail and Soto spun, firing as he turned. His bullets stitched splintery scars across the trees and whizzed away through the fog.

My ears rang with the shots.

"Wait!" I called, straining to regain some of my hearing.

Nothing moved.

Lugo and Soto stood a few feet apart and back-to-back, their weapons at the ready.

I breathed in and breathed out.

They might have just been jumpy.

Or...

Suddenly, the mist parted, and Tobar appeared, like a grim visage of death. He had stripped down to shorts and had painted himself white, like some kind of war paint.

He swung his tomahawk upward.

I was too slow to counter but my sword took the impact. My blade was sent spinning and Tobar kicked me hard in the chest. I was sent sprawling.

As Lugo and Soto both squeezed off shots, Tobar melted into the mist again only to reappear between them. Neither could fire for fear of hitting the other. Tobar had holstered his hatchet and now grabbed both of their guns, breaking them off the straps. Lugo and Soto scattered as Tobar smashed the submachine guns against a tree, rendering them useless.

Melanie had retrieved my sword and made a rush at Tobar. Effortlessly, he dodged her swing and caught her by the throat. I was back on my feet and moving. Melanie, quick thinking as ever, tossed the sword back to me. I caught it by the hilt in midair, readying to strike but Tobar had his tomahawk to Melanie's neck.

I stopped.

"Do not follow me." He said, dragging her back into the fog.

CHAPTER EIGHTEEN

I followed him.

I didn't care about Soto and Lugo, just set off with nothing but the aim of rescuing Melanie in my mind.

I had been so close.

But now I knew where to find him.

I prayed for the fog to lift and miraculously, it began to burn off as I got closer and closer to the sound of the waterfall.

Suddenly, I could see them ahead.

The trail narrowed and the precipice was close, I just needed to get Melanie behind me. Tobar no longer had freedom of movement and couldn't use the cloaking fog to his advantage.

Typically, you're being taken somewhere against your will the best thing to do is to make it as difficult as possible for your captor. Usually in the form of fighting tooth and nail or at the very least making yourself dead weight.

Neither were much of an option against a superhumanly strong villain as Tobar.

I tried to think of something that would get his attention.

"Tobar! Why not take me? You are trying to appease the spirit of Tahquitz. I have seen his sign in the sky. The green meteor."

He stopped and turned, his massive left forearm across Melanie's chest like a meaty seatbelt strap. The tomahawk was in his right.

"You are going to die here. You know that in your heart, you have seen it in your mind's eye."

Tobar's voice carried, but just barely, over the crashing falls.

I said nothing. Just adjusted my grip on the hilt of the sword, aiming the point at my enemy.

"But," he continued, "I cannot say which one of you should live to see what I am going to do the other." He moved his fingers to grip Melanie's chin and cheeks and was about to say more when she made her move.

It wasn't her whole body against his whole body. It wasn't even her whole body against a tiny part of his.

It was just teeth against fingers.

Too easy.

She bit like a ravening wolf onto his thumb. Biting through fingers is like biting through carrots. It's easy to do if you commit.

And she was committed.

Tobar looked nonplussed as Melanie slipped from his grip, spitting out a large index finger.

She ran to me.

I couldn't take time to hug her, just swayed out of her way and whispered, "go" as she shot past me.

I shouldn't have been complaining but if I could have taken my pick, I wish she would have taken his thumb so he wouldn't be able to grip with his left, but beggars cannot be choosers.

He charged, and I ran to meet him. His tomahawk held like he was bunting with a baseball bat. My sword blade met the haft of his hatchet with the clang of metal on metal. He disengaged with a shove and aimed a downward stroke.

With my sword above my head, I parried. Before I could counter, he was slashing towards my midriff. I turned the sword point down so that the blade was parallel to my body just in time and the tomahawk sang off the steel.

Moving away from him, I circled warily, my sword held at the low ready. He watched me appraisingly. I didn't take my eyes off him, but I knew that he was closer to the cliff's edge than I was. I couldn't rely on our relative positions staying the same for long, though, because in any fight, it is easy to reverse the geometry of the fight.

Suddenly, he twirled his tomahawk and came for me. He was fast, incredibly so. I ducked under his first swing and tried to slash his legs out from under him, but he sprang back. My sword was longer than his weapon but, with his wingspan it more than evened out.

I parried another probing strike, followed by a swing of my own aimed diagonally across his body.

But before I could begin the attack, his massive right hand closed on my sword hand holding it immobile. With his left hand, sans index finger, he punched me once, twice. In the chest and face. The air was knocked out of me, and I felt blood spurt from my nose. Staggering backwards, I could see through blurry vision that Tobar was smiling. He spun and backhanded me across the face.

I hit the ground on my left shoulder, using the impact as momentum to roll away. He was toying with me. Which was fine because it would give the others time to escape.

I hoped.

More mist rose from the falls and a sudden breeze carried a curtain of the condensation, enveloping Tobar.

The effect was very nearly mystical.

I backed my way down the trail to where it widened out. I had to readjust my strategy and I was hoping to tangle him up in the trees.

He was completely obscured but I had the dreadful thought that he could still see me.

Then, like a ghost ship out of the fog, Tobar emerged. He swung upwards and though I deflected the swipe, the force of the blow knocked my sword wide. Too late to reset in a defensive position, I stepped back—right into a tree. His follow-up hacking attack was coming in parallel to the ground, right at head height.

I leaned left to get outside the arc of the axe, but the edge caught my right shoulder and cut cleanly along the flesh and scarred the tree behind me.

Blood flowed out and I felt the numb tug of an open wound.

My right arm, my sword arm, was weakened but I held onto the hilt. Before Tobar could attempt another strike, I ran between the trees.

Turning around, I didn't see him pursuing. I didn't see him at all.

Blood ran down my arm and onto my sword. The sense of dread I had felt when he disappeared into the mist returned. I knew he was not supernatural. But he was decidedly preternatural.

The trees were worse than the cliff. At least near the precipice he couldn't get behind me unless he flew like a bird.

Pausing an instant, I broke into a run back towards the waterfall.

When I came out of the trees again, I slid on the shale and there, where he had been standing before with Melanie, was Tobar. His back was to me as he looked down at the roiling water.

"I knew you would return. Like a reckless moth to the eternal flame." He said, and though the crashing water roared, I could hear him clearly. "We are all born in blood and water and we all will die in the same. After I cut out your heart, I will find the rest of them, but you need not fear for them. You will be long gone."

In what I hoped was a surprise blitz, I rushed him, thrusting with my sword point for his substantial center mass.

Parrying my thrust, he sidestepped and had I not skidded to a halt, I would have gone off the ledge. As I slid to a stop, I pivoted and turned my sword raised in defense, just as his hatchet crashed down. The sword blade scraped under the force of the blow and a new chink appeared on the edge. The swing would have cut me in two. Even so, I was forced to a knee. Bracing my other hand on the back of the blade, I tried to push against him, but like a hydraulic press, I felt his crushing power.

The roaring of the waterfall behind me was loud and the spray was wet against the back of my head and arms. Blood welled from my shoulder wound with my exertion and my right hand was going numb fast.

The talisman swung from his neck like a pendulum as he leaned forward, and he smiled his shark smile.

The grit ground under my feet as Tobar pushed further.

I had to time it exactly right.

Whenever you are in a pushing or pulling contest, like a tug-o-war, if you suddenly let go of the rope, or stop exerting force against the opposition, the other guy will invariably fall back, or stumble forward, or lose balance.

Easing up on my resistance, I let him press further, before moving the hilt down and diving to the left.

At the same time, I forced the sword point up with my left hand, and as his head came down, I was rewarded with contact to his right eye.

He released an in-human yowl as the steel furrowed his face from forehead to prominent cheekbone, taking his eye in the process.

But though he stumbled slightly, he didn't fall off the cliff. He hadn't been putting all his weight into his push. He didn't need to.

Before I could get my feet back under me, he swung the axe backhanded and blindly. The flat of the blade took me on the cheek and I staggered back against the rock face.

Tobar was pawing blood from his brow and chin.

This was my chance. I still had the sword, held loosely. I could run him through or simply knock him off the cliff with a shoulder charge. But I hesitated. I had never taken a life and as evil as Tobar was, I didn't feel especially eager to slay him.

Which was fortunate.

Because after a beat, he straightened up, like another mountain peak, and stared down at me from his one good eye. Despite the horrific wound, he seemed implacable, unfazed. He had been hoping that I would rush in.

"Not so reckless then, after all." He sighed, smiling.

Spinning the hatchet, he lunged forward. I met his charge with an upward slash, but not towards Tobar—towards his weapon. My strike surprised him, and as I forced his hatchet wide, I turned my sword back on him. My blade scythed in a flashing arc. Tobar leaned back, out of range. My sword point missing his throat by an inch that might as well have been a mile.

My slashing attack had taken me off-balance and opened me up to a counterattack. I let my own momentum from the swing spin me away, but Tobar's tomahawk caught me across the ribs. Not deep, but it stung and tore my shirt and hot blood flowed.

Rotating around, I fought the urge to drop a hand to my side to keep my ribs inside of me.

Wincing, I bared my teeth, which reminded me of Shadow and so I added a snarl, feeling a little more emboldened.

He flicked the tomahawk back and forth like a serpent's tongue. It was hypnotic and I tried to keep my eyes simultaneously on him and his weapon in an attempt to anticipate his next move.

I blocked his first and second strikes with difficulty, but on the third, he twisted his wrist, spinning my sword and nearly tearing it from my grasp. Only a quick pull backwards on the hilt kept me armed.

He flashed his teeth, circling me like an apex predator. I tracked him with the point of my sword. He spun the tomahawk nonchalantly before crow-hopping towards me and swiping crosswise for my head.

Dodging his attack, I tried a thrust for his abdomen that he deflected, and I narrowly parried his oncoming counter stroke. He hacked again towards my head, like a mad woodsman, intent on deforestation. Ducking, I drew back my sword and stabbed upward. My blade skewered his arm through the meat of the bicep, and he dropped the tomahawk. We were now so close to the precipice that his favored weapon fell away without a sound.

Wrenching and twisting the sword, I freed it like Arthur's Excalibur from the Stone.

Red blood dropped into the dust.

Before he could move, I swung down to cut him across the chest.

In a supreme display of athletic ability, and seemingly supernatural skill, he clapped both hands on the flats of the blade, stopping its deadly parabola.

But not soon enough.

The tip of the sword embedded into the little devil totem, like an axe sunk into a stump.

There was bright green flash, as if a flame had surged to life, then died. Perhaps the sunlight on my sword blade.

This time it was no feigned anguish from Tobar. His intact eye went white as it rolled up and his mouth opened unnaturally wide in a silent scream.

He looked down at his transfixed figurine and his hands fell away from my blade.

I pulled back and the talisman stayed attached to the sword, wedged like a block of firewood on the blade of an axe, and came free from Tobar's neck.

I held the emblem of evil aloft, like one of Captain Moroni's soldiers displaying the severed scalp of Zerahemnah on the point of his sword to the opposing army. Then, unceremoniously, I flicked the blade and the slain ivory devil sailed out into space and tumbled down into the depths.

Tobar seemed to shrink. Not completely, but suddenly he seemed smaller. Greatly diminished. No longer a looming figure of evil. Just another run-of-the-mill enemy in a long line of enemies.

Rotating my blade around to point at him and breathing heavily, I waited. He still seemed in shock at the loss of his security blanket, his power source, if such it was. The thundering stampede of the waterfall seemed louder than ever, and he turned, fearfully, to look at the tons upon tons of water as if noticing the cascade for the first time.

From down the trail I sensed more than heard the return of Melanie, Lugo and Soto.

"Hold on everyone, it's over. I got him." I said over my shoulder.

Tobar stared down at the ground, swaying slightly and bleeding from his arm, hand, and face.

"It's over, Tobar. Give up. You've met your master."

His gaze turned on me and though I saw real fear in his remaining eye, there was something else. Something shadowy and incorporeal. Something moving behind the curtains. Like an invisible predator stalking through the grasslands that bends the stalks where it walks.

"Yes." His voice was no longer as monstrously imposing. Just hoarse. "I *have* met my master and now you will as well."

He wasn't going to come quietly. That was for sure. But I wasn't about to murder an unarmed man.

On the other hand, there was a score to settle.

Spinning the sword in a fast figure eight in front of me, I moved forward. Tobar spread his arms, as though he were expecting death, maybe even welcoming it. But instead, I used the momentum of my movement to bury the sword deep in the earth next to me, like King Arthur in reverse.

Stepping away from my blade, I smiled and raised my fists.

Tobar looked from the sword and then to me. He returned my smile with one of his own—a smile that was all teeth and no heart, spreading wide as the gates of hell.

Maybe this was a mistake.

Behind me, Melanie and Lugo and Soto were drawing nearer.

Without looking back, I held up my right fist at a right angle, an infantry signal to hold up. "Let me handle this, guys."

As weakened and demoralized as he should have been, he wasn't finished. With lightning speed, he closed the distance from me, grabbing for my neck. Batting his hands away with my left, I snapped a thunderous right cross to the center of his face. It was like punching not-quite-dry cement. He didn't slow his charge and as we collided, I skidded backwards on my heels. He changed targets, reaching instead for my wounded shoulder. Needles of fire cartwheeled through my nervous system as he dug his fingers into the cut. I yelled in pain and responded in kind with a pair of uppercuts to his punctured arm.

His grip relaxed and as we disengaged, he punched me once, twice in the face. They were weak and off-balanced blows, otherwise they might have killed me.

Thankfully, they only sent me stumbling back several yards and left my head spinning. He followed after me, winding up and throwing a backhanded swipe towards my face.

Slipping underneath it, I launched forward, butting him under the chin. I heard his teeth clack together, but his head barely budged back. His neck must have been like an iron bar. In rapid succession, I slammed a series of short punches to his ribs with insignificant effect.

Grunting, he grabbed hold of both my arms and lifted me bodily into the air. Twisting like an Olympian hurling a discus, he threw me over the edge of the cliff.

For a terrible instant, I hung above the void. The sound of rushing water in my ears, in my bones. I looked down all two hundred feet to the roiling river below.

Then I caught hold of Tobar's wrist. His arms were still extended from tossing me and, like Tarzan, I swung back from the fall. I ended up behind Tobar, locking my legs in a figure four around his middle. I got an arm under his chin, and another behind his head in a rear naked choke. He was bleeding from his face and the coppery, sticky blood covered me as well.

Squeezing for all I was worth. I felt his sinews and tendons bunch beneath me. Any normal person would have been asleep in seconds, but his neck was so thick that I could neither cut off his carotid arteries, nor crush his windpipe.

He clawed at me, his feet shifting beneath him for balance. Melanie, Lugo, and Soto were disregarding my directions and moving towards us now. Tobar dug his chin down and tried to peel my arm from his neck, but when he saw the three of them closing in, he stretched forth his left hand like an insistent traffic cop and uttered a gurgling roar from his throat.

Incredibly, there was a rumble and even though I was hanging on like a backpack and didn't have my feet on the ground, I felt the vibrations from the earth travel up from Tobar's feet and nearly rattle me off. Loose shale and small rocks skittered along the trail, and then a pair of huge rocks tumbled down. Lugo cried out and grabbed Melanie, just before she could be crushed by the surprise rockslide.

They were stuck on the other side of the trail, until they could clear the rocks or climb over them.

My legs were tiring quickly. My right arm was almost entirely numb. My wounds stung from sweat and the blood between us was mingling with the dust, covering us in a viscous mixture.

Tobar seemed to stagger but stayed upright. Swinging into the rock face, he tried to scrape me off. Then he slammed himself backwards, once, twice, thrice. I thought my back would be broken as he pancaked me, and I knew I would not make it through another crushing impact like that.

The effort seemed to have sapped him of his strength, but I was fading too. It was just a matter of time before he either succumbed to my submission attempt or beat me once and for all.

I was losing my grip, and I didn't think I had anything left for a last stand. I had wanted to incapacitate and capture Tobar. I hadn't wanted to kill him. I still didn't. Not even out of self-defense.

Again, he slammed me against the wall.

I felt something inside me break loose.

A rib?

Perhaps a handful.

Nobody lives forever.

I figured this was as good a way to go as any; locked in epic combat with a worthy adversary.

His hands reached back, and I pressed my face against the back of his head to protect my eyes from prying fingers. We struggled against each other, each summoning the last dregs of strength and will.

From the other side of the rockslide, I heard a bark, an exclamation, and something scrabbling over loose rocks.

There was Shadow, in all his snarling fury.

He bolted for us, hackles raised, his maw opening as wide as Fenris wolf swallowing the sun.

My grip slipped and Tobar wrenched my arm from his neck. One massive hand seized my wrist, and he turned his head raising a forearm as Shadow leapt with a snarl.

It looked like Shadow was going for the proffered appendage like those police dogs do in training, but at the last instant he ducked under, and his fangs closed on Tobar's throat, right where my own arm had been moments before.

Shadow planted all four paws onto the giant of a man, and for a second stood vertically, then Shadow leapt back, as if from a springboard, launching off Tobar's chest. He landed upright and ready, but out of reach of Tobar.

I was not so fortunate.

Now grievously wounded, Tobar arched his back, clutching at his torn jugular with one hand, my wrist still clamped in the other. Arterial blood flowed freely like a fountain. He lost balance and stepped backwards.

Into nothing.

He swayed for a moment, and I thought he was going to make it, but maybe it was my added weight on his back, or the injuries, or the loss of his totem, but whatever it was, we fell.

We did a full backflip and I pushed off and away from Tobar. I couldn't hear his scream because the waterfall was deafening. Or maybe because of his wound he was unable to make a sound.

We were suspended in a rushing world of white water and spray and sound.

One, one thousand.

I had dived off cliffs into calm water before, but nothing over sixty feet.

Two one thousand.

The principle had to be the same, though. I was vertical, in a T-shape. Tobar looked like a skydiver without a parachute. Spread-eagled.

Three one thousand.

I squeezed my legs together and brought my arms tight against me, closed my eyes and braced for impact.

Four one thou---.

We hit the water, and I sliced right through. I sank all the way to the bottom and felt the tremendous weight of water churning above my head, and the rough stones below my feet. The bubbles swirled all around me. I pushed up but had only just broken the surface and gulped a bit of air before the current swirled me under and rattled me down the river.

I saw no sign of Tobar. Maybe like the Wicked Witch of the West he had simply melted upon contact with the water.

That would have explained his aversion to it.

I popped up again like a cork and maneuvered to my back, pointing my feet downstream to ward off any rocks or debris in my path. I bounced like a pinball through a series of rapids, feeling like a forgotten quarter clattering around in a washing machine.

I went under again, spun around before knocking against something large that was floating along with me.

Tobar.

Face down. Unmoving.

Draping myself over him, I flutter kicked out of the main current to where the stream shallowed and I steered us into a little eddy.

I wanted to roll him over, check for signs of life, give him CPR if need be. But I was suddenly disoriented and unsteady. My shoulder and side ached terribly, the pain scything through the fog in my head. It was broad daylight, but my vision was going dark. I fell to my knees in the sandy bank. Pitching forward on my face next to Tobar and slept the sleep of the dead.

CHAPTER NINETEEN

It might have been Heaven. But it didn't feel quite like I thought it would.

It was cool and dark. It smelled of woodsmoke and broiling meat and sounded of a crackling fire overlaid with all the night sounds of the forest; wind in the trees, insects, birds. I rolled over onto my side, finding myself covered in an old army blanket.

I scooched up into a sitting position and saw Lark sitting on a log on the other side of the fire. She was forking a couple of thick steaks onto a pair of enameled plates. She had her shotgun and rifle close to hand and the bowie knife hanging in a shoulder scabbard.

"You're awake, well, it's about time. You don't snore though, in case you ever wondered. Now, before you ask me a slew of questions, the girls are fine. Melanie got them and they met up with the search parties. She told them they would have to come back for you in a helicopter. They should pick you up by morning."

I tried to stand but still felt a little woozy.

"My face hurts."

"It's killing me, too." She laughed.

I reached up to touch my nose that must have been damaged by Tobar's punches.

"Don't touch it, it's broken." She said.

I took her advice.

"Hungry?" She asked.

I actually had to think about it. "Yes. Yes, I am."

The more I moved the more I realized just how stiff and sore and bruised I was. I glanced down at my shoulder. My t-shirt sleeve had been rolled up and there was a rough stitching job where the wound had been.

"What did you use to sew me up, bootlaces?" I asked.

She grinned her big smile. "Fishing line, but I can tear them out and let you do it yourself if it isn't to your liking."

"Maybe later."

With my good arm I took the steak and said a silent prayer over it before I ate.

I was several bites deep before I looked up. "Tobar washed up next to me on the shore. Did you do anything with the body?"

She shrugged. "We only found you on the riverbank, me and Shadow that is. He sniffed around a bit but there was neither hide nor hair of that fella."

"I thought I had got him far enough onto the bank before I blacked out, but he must have gotten caught by the current and floated away."

She chewed on her steak, spat a bit of gristle into the fire and listened to it sizzle, paused a beat before looking out into the woods.

"Must have." She said, like she wasn't entirely convinced.

I didn't press the matter and neither did she.

But it was something to think about.

Could he have survived?

I looked around the campsite she had made. We were in between a cluster of several large trees in a wide clearing, a sort of meadow with tall grasses and wildflowers. The river was not more than a hundred yards away. The open field would make a good landing spot for the chopper. Lark really did know these mountains.

"Where is my faithful hound anyway?"

Lark shrugged and gestured at the forest with her two-tined fork. "He'll be off galivanting across the mountains I imagine. He stuck around long enough for me to assure him you were going to pull through, then he just disappeared."

I was a little crestfallen at that, but I tried not to let it show.

"Thank you, Lark, for everything."

"I started that book of yorn."

"I'm glad to hear it." I said.

"I got to ask you something, though."

"Shoot."

"Do Laman and Lemuel ever figure it out?"

I smiled. "You'll just have to keep reading."

"Oh, I intend to."

We ate our steaks and shared a canteen of cold water. The sparks from the fire wafted up and disappeared but the stars stood out brighter.

It was a clear night and I felt like I could see from one end of Heaven to the other. We saw a few scattered satellites which seemed to mar the natural order, but we also counted several shooting stars which only enhanced it.

Thankfully none of them had a green tint to them.

"What will you do now, Sawyer?"

"What do you mean?"

"You don't want to go back to civilization any more than I do. You hate the press of people and the noise and the skyscrapers. I can see it in you. You're not a half-bad woodsman. I can see that, too. You could survive up here."

I didn't say anything. Mostly because she was right.

"But on the other hand, that is quite a woman you've got. It would be a shame to lose her, and I can't imagine her wanting to rough it in the wilds indefinitely."

I breathed out a long exhalation. "I don't know. I think there is something in between. There are plenty of small towns out there without high-rises and as for the people, they aren't all bad, you know. In fact, they are mostly good. I can count the truly evil people that I've met on one hand. There are more good people—like you—than you might think."

She sucked her teeth, staring into the fire before looking across to me.

"Maybe, Sawyer. Maybe someday I'll wander down from these hills and buy a soda from a gas station and sit in a restaurant."

"You could come to Church with me." I suggested.

Her smile widened and I was reminded just how pretty a good smile is.

"You ever keep bees?" She asked.

"Nope, my uncle in Wisconsin does, though."

"My father was a beekeeper, best darned honey you ever tasted. But one time he tried to move a hive that had settled on a well cover. I remember that mass of bees lifting off like a cloud and turning in the air all in unison, like a flock of birds, before taking off across the sky.

We held out hope that they would come back but once disturbed, they don't often return.

I think you're like those bees. You get comfy but as soon as someone tries to move you—disturbs you—you will be long gone, off to who knows where. Me, well, I'm different than most folks and different from you. I like my roots, I like staying put, but I can be transplanted. You can't be planted at all. You're a regular old tumbleweed. A gunslinger who rides out of town after the shootout."

"You make it sound so romantic." I said.

"Romantic?" She spat into the fire. "Ain't nothing romantic about nature. But there is beauty in it, I suppose. Purpose. Meaning. Satisfaction. That is better than romance. You are a born wanderer. You can't change that."

"Read a little bit more of the Book of Mormon and you will read about Lehi teaching his sons about agency, about how we are to act, not be acted upon. All of us can change."

She nodded sagely. "To be sure, all of us can change, but you aren't ever going to want to. You're a locomotive, an unstoppable force and all you can do is keep moving forward, furiously laying the tracks down with no set direction. Why do you think Shadow took off? You and he were pals but you're both lone wolves."

I smiled a little sheepishly, "bees, gunfighters, trains, and wolves. You know how to flatter a guy—and thank you—for the compliments."

"I don't know that I did compliment you, more like commenting on my observations is all."

"Well, thanks all the same. I'm really not sure what the future holds, but I look forward to it."

"None of us is sure of what the future holds." She said. "It's like those magicians, who fan out a bunch of cards and tell you to pick one. And if the cards are all against you, just reshuffle the lot of them."

She took a long drink of water and ran a hand across her mouth and down her throat. "Land sakes, I ain't talked this much in a coon's age. Enough to make a body hoarse. You better get some sleep. Melanie will be back at first light with that helo for you."

I was just getting started. It was nice to talk to someone without any filters or devices. Someone whose brain didn't break when confronted with any sort of real opinion, and she had plenty of her own. But her suggestion of sleep was like a horse tranquilizer and suddenly I felt very tired.

I yawned and lay down by the fire and for the first time in a long time, I didn't dream.

The next thing I heard was the thrum of the rotors and I opened my eyes to the morning sun. The fire was out but still smoking faintly. Lark was gone without a trace.

All her equipment, even my blanket, was gone. Stiffly, I rose to my feet. Every part of me felt like it had been contorted, wrung out, and run over. My knee still twinged from my first fall off a cliff. I couldn't raise my right arm.

Shuffling out from beneath the tree cover, I waved my good hand at the approaching helicopter. It was a Bell 205 with San Diego County Sheriff decals. It circled until the pilot found a suitable spot and touched down in the meadow. The tall grass rolled like waves on the sea. Melanie and some sort of official rescue person spilled out of the doorway and ran to me.

I must have looked even worse than I felt because as she drew near Melanie burst into tears and embraced me.

I caught a glimpse of my bruised and cut face in the other guy's tinted glasses, as he moved to put one of my arms over his shoulder. I was about to tell them that I didn't need any help when my knee buckled, and I stumbled.

We all ducked under the rotor wash, and they helped me get strapped in. We took off and I saw the mountains and the meadows, and the trees roll by beneath us. I saw the river and the waterfall.

I had never been in a helicopter before.

I would not recommend it.

If I had been nauseous before, I would have been as green as grass after a few minutes.

I closed my eyes and Melanie squeezed my right hand. It was loud in the cabin, and I didn't feel like talking. I reached up and, disregarding Lark's counsel, tried to assess my nose's damage. Stars burst behind my eyes, and I must have passed out again.

CHAPTER TWENTY

It certainly wasn't Heaven; of that I was for sure.

But it was bright and white. It smelled of disinfectant and the fluorescent tube lighting sounded like a beehive without honey. There seemed to be a lot of expensive-looking equipment beeping next to me, which didn't help me in my efforts to go back to sleep. An IV dripped something into the back of my hand.

I am very grateful for modern medicine and for hard-working nurses and doctors who know so much more than I do about the bodies God gave us. But I have always been a little ill-at-ease in hospitals. As a missionary in Peru, I had seen some pretty dismal clinics that had not inspired much confidence.

At least my room here had a window. It was a bright, clear day and even though I couldn't feel the breeze, I saw the treetops swaying lazily.

I figured the time was early afternoon.

Even with the IV, I was thirsty. I looked around for a bottle of water, or something. I was glad that nobody had brought flowers or balloons or bears. I didn't want to make a big deal about my convalescence.

There was no water bottle, or cup of ice chips.

I ran a hand over my jaw and felt a substantial growth of beard, I hadn't shaved since the day we had left on the camping trip.

Felt like a lifetime ago.

Yawning, I let my eyes close, and I was back asleep before I knew it.

A smiling nurse carrying a clipboard came and checked on me. She asked me something and I must have responded because she nodded and made a note.

She went away and I fell asleep again, still thirsty.

A shadow fell across the open doorway, and I opened my eyes.

Tobar stood there, leaning against the doorframe, his massive arms folded across his refrigerator-sized chest. Thankfully, he was unarmed. He wasn't covered in warpaint anymore and was wearing a smock the color of buckskin. Predictably, he said nothing, just stared unblinking with both eyes.

Both eyes?

I looked to see if his left pointer finger had regenerated but I couldn't tell from the way he had his arms crossed.

His countenance seemed to have softened somewhat. As though the pounding cascades had shorn the hard edges from off his face, smoothed them like river rocks.

I wanted to tell him that I was sorry it had to end that way. That I was sorry he was dead, having been so unprepared to meet God.

But I didn't.

"See you around." I said, closing my eyes.

When I opened them again, he had gone away. Hopefully forever. I had seen enough of Wendigos to last a lifetime. Several lifetimes, in fact.

I must have dozed off again.

Later, Melanie came to see me. She looked great in low-cut jeans, and she was wearing a t-shirt that said, "Granite Mountain Movie Club Podcast," whatever that was.

She had a funny look on her face and while she was visibly relieved that I was alive and kicking, or at least sitting up, there was something between us that I couldn't put my finger on.

She did, though, quite literally.

After she kissed my forehead, she stepped back and pulled my things out of her pocket. My passport, my cash, and the ring that I had fashioned from a quarter. Most quarters prior to 1970 had been made with silver.

"I didn't take you for much of a jewelry guy," she said.

I felt my face flush, just a little. I am not given to embarrassment but blushing easily is a sign of an honest person, or so I've heard.

"I'm not." I said.

"Then what's it for? Who's it for?"

I said nothing.

She softened a little and sighed, reaching her hands out for mine.

I gripped them both with my right hand, the one without tubes and wires.

She bit her lip and shook her head, sort of hiding a smile. "You sweet, silly boy. We never even talked about it. What was your plan?"

"Oh, I pretty much just make things up as I go along." I said.

"So, are you going to ask me?"

"Ask you what?"

She raised her eyebrow at me. "Now you're playing dumb?"

"Whose playing?" I said, smiling. "They've got me on all sorts of painkillers, I'm probably delirious."

She looked at me deeply. "Nice try, your eyes are clear, and I know that you always refuse all medicines for pain."

"Yeah, I'm kind of a glutton for punishment."

"I'll say." She smiled and sat down on the edge of my bed.

"Hey, I just remembered, are the Ayres okay?"

She nodded, "you wouldn't believe it, it took them so long because their car broke down before they got to cell service. It was too far and too steep for them to walk back so they just kept walking down the road until they got some bars."

"Tell me what happened, after Tobar and I went swimming."

"We couldn't get to the cliff because of the rockslide but we saw you both falling. I, I don't even want to remember it. Oh, Sawyer, I thought I was going to have to watch you die. But then Soto saw you swimming way far away, and I know how good you are in the water, so I wasn't as worried."

"How did you get to the girls?"

"Shadow led us back through the cave."

"Really? I'm surprised Lugo made it through the tight spots."

"There weren't any tight spots, it was like a walk in the park, just straight through."

"What? You didn't find a big antechamber with the makings of a campfire?"

"No, we didn't."

"I must have taken a wrong turn. Okay, so what about Lark?"

She looked confused. "Who's Lark?"

"The hermit lady. The one whose cabin the girls were in."

She put a hand on my forehead.

"Are you sure you're feeling okay?"

"She was the one who got me off the riverbank and built the fire and cooked me steak. She was the one who sewed up my shoulder."

"Sawyer," she said slowly, "there was no one there. Your shoulder wasn't stitched until we got you here."

I looked at the wound.

Neat medical stitches, not the fishing line I remembered.

"Okay, but the girls saw her. I left them under her care, hers and Shadow's when I came to find you."

She shook her head. "The girls were by themselves. The cabin was well-provisioned but very old. The forest rangers had no idea it was even there."

I was growing less sure of myself. "But the girls saw me talking to her. She was the one who gave me the sword, there were a bunch of weapons."

"Ashlin said that you had been talking to Shadow, but that's all, they thought it was a little odd. There were no weapons in the cabin unless you count canned peaches as part of an arsenal." She was smiling and even if she didn't mean it to look condescending, that was what it felt like.

I put my head back on my thin pillow. "Maybe I'm going crazy."

"Is this an elaborate way of getting out of popping the question?"

"You've had to testify in court, right? As part of your deputy duties?"

She nodded.

"Then you probably know the old trial lawyer adage, not to ask a question that you don't already know the answer to."

"Yes," she said slowly.

"Well, I don't know what your answer would be. If I asked you to marry me. And either way, I'm not sure that I want to know. These last few days were revealing of my inability to protect you. And that frightens me more than anything.

You have a great job, and you're so good at it. I don't even have a steady income. How could I provide for you? What kind of paperwork even goes into a marriage license? There are way more kidnappings going on in the world and you and I aren't always there to stop them. I love you, Melanie, but I can't endanger you. There are always going to be bad guys out there and they can never show up at my front door if I don't have a front door."

She opened her mouth to respond when there was a rap at the door and a gruff, insincere throat-clearing.

We looked up to see two men in suits and ties standing shoulder to shoulder.

Melanie stood up.

"I hope we're not interrupting, Deputy Clark."

"No, please come in, gentlemen." She said.

You darn well are interrupting. I thought

They shuffled in and cast about as if looking for a place to sit down, but then thought better of it and stood shoulder to shoulder.

The guy who had spoken first looked expectantly at Melanie. She hesitated, pursed her lips and said, "I'll be back."

Then she was gone. Just like Tobar but hopefully not forever.

"What are you guys, Candy Stripers?" I asked.

"Funny man." The first guy said. He was lean and weasel-like, with a face like an inverted triangle and hooded eyes that gave him the flavor of a hippie. He had the makings of stubble and a cheap haircut.

He seemed full of nervous energy, shifting his weight from foot to foot, bouncing and looking all around.

"We're federal agents." The second guy said. He was a youngish, rotund man with rosy cheeks and a pinched face. His voice was more high-pitched than I would have expected. He seemed on edge as well, but his discomfort manifested itself in the form of a constant wringing of his hands as though he were washing them.

I smiled sardonically, said nothing.

The first guy pulled a badge wallet out, making sure I saw the shoulder holster and Glock 19. Which made me smile more. It wasn't wise to show your hand right away and his attempt at intimidation had been poorly timed and overplayed.

I am naturally inclined to be skeptical of government officials, or government anything for that matter, but I wanted to give them the benefit of every single doubt. Maybe their manner was just a lack of confidence in themselves and not outright incompetence.

"I'm Special Agent Russell Lovelett, and this is Special Agent Jeremy Fuller." The weasel guy said.

"Okay."

"We've got some questions for you." He said, looking everywhere but at me.

"Shoot."

Lovelett licked his lips, putting his hands on his hips, which slowed the rocking from foot to foot. "Actually, it's more of a message."

I waited, noticing that there hadn't been any preamble. No small talk, no inquiries as to how I was recovering. Not that I wanted them to be my Valentine or anything, but their lack of bedside manners was appalling.

"We have talked to all the kids, and to Deputy Clark, but we wanted to run our...assessment by you first, as evidently you were the most closely involved."

I kept waiting.

He continued. "We know what you think happened up on the mountain. You and those girls went on a hike, got lost, and suffered from severe dehydration, which led to some pretty intense delirium and hallucinations, not uncommon at all."

I narrowed my eyes. Kept waiting.

Agent Fuller jumped in. "We have a departmental psychologist standing by to counsel the young ladies."

I looked from one to the other, hardly believing what I was hearing.

Agent Lovelett tapped his feet. "We think it is better for all concerned if we don't make a big thing out of this."

"All concerned being the two of you?" I asked.

Agent Fuller moved closer alongside my bed. "Listen, Sawyer, if we don't play our cards right then this will be front page news. An international incident. We've got a lot of factors to consider. This could end up affecting foreign policy. You know what a hot topic the Mexican border is right now. We'll be up to our ears in issues."

"That's what you guys signed up for, isn't it?" I asked.

Agent Lovelett patted the air, trying to calm the tide of tension. He exchanged a look with Fuller. "Mr. Sawyer, we apologize. We know you have sustained serious injuries. How are you feeling, by the way?"

I should have seen the trap, but I didn't.

"Great. Fine. Dandy. One hundred percent." I said.

The pair swapped another glance.

Fuller smiled and shook his head making a *tsk, tsk* sound. "That is not what the doctors said, Sawyer. You got beat up good. You're lucky to be alive. I can see just by looking at you that your nose won't be the same again. You're going to have some scars. Your knee is in bad shape."

"I feel fine." I said again.

Lovelett grinned at me. "You know that it is a crime to make false statements to us, right? You just lied to us about your physical state. We could charge you."

Fuller jumped in as though on cue. "Unless you're willing to play ball. We're of the mind that if there is no harm, then there is no foul. All those girls are safe and sound, that's all that matters, right? Who cares what the narrative is?"

It actually made some kind of sense. I like things off the record. Like Melanie had said, I prefer no paperwork.

I nodded slowly.

Lovelett looked relieved. "So, we're in agreement then? Nothing happened up on the mountain."

I held up a finger. "Except it did. And it will again, somewhere, unless the two of you start doing your jobs."

Fuller shook his head. "I'll try and make this as monosyllabic as possible. Nothing happened up in the mountains."

"That was nine syllables long."

He clapped his hands together, exasperatedly. "Listen, wise guy. We have seen things you couldn't imagine. You have to listen to us on this. It's the best way forward."

These were impatient federal agents.

"Is this why Melanie couldn't stay?" I asked.

Lovelett exhaled exasperatedly. "Deputy Clark already gave us her statement. The victims already gave us their statements.

We are corroborating those statements to fit the timeline and to be frank you are now the fly in the ointment. You are unestablished here in the community. No fixed address, no work history, no property."

"No taxes." Fuller chimed.

"No taxes." Lovelett said with gravity.

"So what? That makes me an unreliable witness?" I asked.

"As a matter of fact, yes. And worse than that, in addition to the charges for your false statements earlier about your physical condition, who's to say that you weren't the one who kidnapped the girls? Who's to say that you weren't conspiring with those guys? You see, Sawyer, we're giving you a choice. You either toe the line like everyone else will, or we can hang this around your head. You're looking at a potential murder charge once we find that body of Tobar's. Double homicide when we include Mr. Stanislav. Not to mention further obstruction of justice, aiding and abetting for letting Lugo and Soto go."

I laughed. "What is this bad cop, worse cop?"

"Where are Lugo and Soto?" Lovelett asked.

"Let me ask you guys a question. How did this happen? How is it that your government agencies were twiddling their thumbs while three foreign nationals waltzed into America to traffic in young girls? I did your job for you, you should be giving me an award and naming a building after me, but luckily for you I am not into that kind of thing, I'm happy to let you two take the credit. But instead, you two want to try and intimidate me, railroad me, scapegoat me? Well, you go ahead and try."

Lovelett exchanged a look with Fuller, then slowly smiled. "Alright, Sawyer, let's say we go with your story. What are your plans once you leave the hospital?"

"You mean what kind of a kerfuffle am I going to stir up with the media."

He made a sarcastic, sweeping, concessionary gesture.

"Whether or not you agree with me, you can't hurt me. You can't scare me. I'm not out to publicize myself. I'm not looking for a book deal or movie rights or commendations. I'm not even looking to get you fired. You guys dropped the ball and fortunately there are people like Melanie and me who'll pick it up."

Lovelett's face twisted and Fuller looked away.

"Melanie, huh? You two are together? That doesn't look good for her. A deputy dating a dubious drifter. That might hurt her career advancement. In fact, we could make sure it does. She could lose her job. How does that make you feel? That she wouldn't be able to show her face around town."

The EKG machine started beeping faster.

Russell snapped his fingers and made a mock-pensive motion with his hand on his chin.   Now there is a good headline. A scandal involving a deputy sheriff's anti-government boyfriend."

I balled my hands into fists, leaning forward on my hospital bed.

"Is this what you guys do all day? Figure out how to ruin the lives of American citizens to cover your own hides?"

Lovelett held up his hands. "We're just looking for a little cooperation. We need to know that you are going to play ball. This could be the best-case scenario ever, Sawyer, we really lucked out with none of your group getting killed but if we blow this out of proportion then we won't be able to take care of more important business behind the scenes."

"I don't believe for a second that you two are interested in anything more than pushing pencils until pension time."

"So that's a no?" Lovelett asked.

"That's a no." I nodded.

Fuller kneaded his hands together. "Very well, Sawyer. You leave us no choice but to bring charges against you."

The EKG monitor slowed.

"I'm way past listening, fellas, so now it's your turn. I can sort of understand not wanting to draw too much attention to the breach in the border, I can relate to wanting to circumvent certain protocols. But you guys showed me that you're not taking this seriously the moment you suggested turning this cover up into a frame up. You've got nothing to worry about from me. Like I said, I'm not interested in fame or fortune. But if I don't see something in the papers about you cracking down on the human trafficking going on under your noses..."

Lovelett held up a finger and pulled out a slim folder.

"Let me stop your little tirade right there, Sawyer. We almost forgot. Do you remember another mess you got yourself into in Peru?"

I paused. "There were a few."

He tossed the folder onto my lap.

I opened it and saw the face of Kucera staring back at me from what might have been a passport photograph.

Lovelett spoke, "Interpol had been after that guy. He had murdered women and children in Bolivia and Chile. Not the brightest operator in the business but proficient enough to make a good living harvesting organs."

"I know." I said.

Fuller picked up where his partner had left off, "his accomplice in Peru thought their scheme was just for ransom. They hadn't expected some bible-thumping kid to start snooping. But you did and everyone went home happy."

Lovelett chimed in, "except Kucera. Which you well know since you're the one who killed him."

I interrupted, "I didn't kill him."

"You dropped him down a chasm."

I frowned. "Proverbs, chapter twenty-six, verse twenty-seven; 'whoso diggeth a pit shall fall therein'. The Book of Mormon says, 'that great pit which hath been digged for the destruction of men shall be filled by those who digged it, unto their utter destruction'. It seems to me that Kucera signed his own death warrant."

Lovelett motioned to the folder, and I turned the page. There was another photograph of someone else. He had Kucera's looks but was younger, fatter, with a shiny shaved head, a mustache, and gold earrings.

"That is not how his brother feels about it." Lovelett said. "Kucera was the black sheep in a serious crime family. Everyone else was organized, Kucera was sadistic, impulsive, a loose cannon. You did them a favor, really. He was a liability, but he was also family. They were involved, tangentially, with the Haitians and the Mexicans, so learning that you not only have been a thorn in their side recently but that you're the same one who killed Kucera. They want you bad, Sawyer."

I remembered hearing from Lugo that there were worse people than the Haitians who were after me.

Lovelett took the folder back from me.

"Would you like to reassess your position now, tough guy?"

I said nothing.

Fuller and Lovelett smiled, sensing the tide turning.

A young nurse, or intern or whatever wearing a medical mask came in pushing a cart. She shooed out the special agents. She started fiddling with the machines and making marks on a clipboard.

"We'll see you soon, Sawyer." Lovelett called over his shoulder. I heard their shoes squeak down the hall.

The nurse turned to me and pulled down her mask.

It was Kami.

"Hi Brother Sawyer."

"What are you doing here?" I asked, leaning forward, and looking out the door to make sure the agents didn't catch her.

"We all came to bring you a get-well-soon card and some treats. Sister Clark said you needed help, and she swiped these scrubs from the laundry."

She indicated the cart. "Melanie said you'd need clothes." She moved out of the room and closed the door. Swinging my legs to the floor, I pulled off the tubes and wires and things that connected me to the expensive machinery. There was a pair of crisp new jeans and a long-sleeved white shirt with three buttons at the top. She had also supplied me with a pair of tube socks and a pair of Lincoln boots from Origin, Maine.

Dressing as quickly as I could without tearing any stitches, I left the hospital gown on the floor and pocketed my effects that Melanie had left on the bedside. Putting my ear to the door, I listened for any sound of the special agents in the hallway. Hearing nothing, I slipped out the door.

Kami had gone.

Walking down the hall in a casual, albeit somewhat limping manner, I nodded to the nurse at the station. She was simultaneously on the phone and on a computer and didn't notice me. Stopping at the bank of elevators, I hit the down button but then took the stairs.

Always take the stairs.

If the special agents were downstairs, they might be distracted by the arriving elevator.

The ground floor door had a wired glass window, and I could see several people moving about. I saw the girls with a couple balloons and paper plates wrapped in plastic. Then, by the lobby doors, I saw Melanie talking to Lovelett and Fuller. Their backs were to me, and Melanie made no sign that she had seen me, except for a split-second raise of her eyebrow as her gaze passed from one agent to the other.

I waved and she brought her left hand to her brow like she was moving an errant strand of hair away.

She was wearing the ring.

I felt a deep longing in my heart and a warm but hollow feeling in the pit of my stomach. What a dream it would be. She was perfect. And while I wasn't going to lament my own decision with a lot of nonsense about noble sacrifices or self-deprecation, I did miss her already.

I followed the stairs down to the underground parking lot, each step echoing.

The what ifs will tear you apart.

Melanie had given me a way out from the constricting bind of the boa constrictor-like bureaucratic red-tape. For that I was grateful. She had given me her heart and had taken mine and like the pea in a shell-game, all the shuffling had left me unsure as to whose was which and where they were.

I tend to steer clear of emotionally based decisions. Nevertheless, they always seem to present themselves. I also try to avoid other things that still encroach under the guise of absolute, glittering necessity, like credit cards, favorite sports teams, insurance programs, retirement benefits, investment accounts, television sets, videogame consoles, streaming subscriptions, mortgages, antiperspirants, Teflon cookware, political parties, homeowners' associations, refined sugars, microplastics, the food pyramid, 24-hour news cycles, and smart phones.

I walked among the vehicles until I came to the ramp that let out into the warm sunny day.

There was hardly any traffic, and I wasn't sure where I was going. But there were evildoers out there, doing evil and I figured preventative maintenance is better than reactionary repair work.

I walked out onto the shoulder of the highway and looked left, looked right, and started walking, slowly at first, until the pain in my knee dulled, then with longer strides. I kept going until I was in a lumbering run.

I wasn't sure when, but I knew, without a shadow of a doubt, that I would be back.

ABOUT THE AUTHOR

All you really need to know about Brett Cain is that he is your friend and that he loves you. He loves everyone and he loves fighting.

He has lived a lot of what he writes and looks forward to many more extraordinary experiences for such an ordinary man.

Brett would enjoy hearing from his readers. You can write to him at brettcainbooks@gmail.com and follow him on X (formerly Twitter) @BrettWCain

Brett lives in Northern California with his wife and daughter.

Brett Cain

Made in the USA
Monee, IL
20 January 2024

52095255R00111